THE COLDEST SAVAGE STOLE MY HEART

J. DOMINIQUE

Cole Hart
SIGNATURE NOVELS

Mailing List

To stay up to date on new releases, plus get information on contests, sneak peeks, and more,

Go To The Website Below...

WWW.COLEHARTSIGNATURE.COM

NIVEA

"*Y*ou a bitch ass nigga, Ky. I swear to God you ain't shit!" I fumed as I stood outside the door of my baby daddy's house. I'd come over on the way home from work to see if he would help me buy our daughter, Kymia, some shoes. At fourteen, she was growing out of her shoes damn near every month and even with two jobs, I couldn't keep up. It had taken a lot to swallow my pride and come to him for help knowing that there was a chance he would tell me no. He'd never really helped out when it came to her expenses, and when I was pregnant at fifteen, I had a ton of excuses for him. Fourteen years later, I could no longer let the shit go. How could I when I was barely hanging on and could count on one hand the things that he'd provided her with since she'd been born?

"Get the fuck away from my door, bitch! Go ask yo' other baby daddy to help you! My girl on her way right now and you better hope I don't make her beat yo' ass for talkin' that slick shit!" He barked back, but I bet his ass ain't open the door and say that shit to my face.

"Fuck you! Yo' ass wasn't thinking 'bout her when you

1

was just trying to get some in exchange for some damn shoes!" I shouted and kicked the wooden door as hard as I could.

Tears burned my eyes threatening to fall at any moment, but I wiped them away. I wasn't getting emotional about the things that he was saying or even how he was treating me. Hell, I was used to this from Kymere. Since I'd told him I was pregnant, he went through fazes where he completely denied our baby. Right now, seemed to be one of them.

Now, I was on the verge of tears because I was angry. Angry at myself for coming here, and angry for being in a situation that forced me to come. I ignored the stares and laughter from the nosy ass people on his block as I hit the door one last time and turned to leave. I could still hear him yelling out idle threats behind the safety of the door, but I was done entertaining him and his neighbors for the day. Screeching tires and the slamming of car doors made me look up from the ground to see Ky's latest girlfriend, Pumpkin, stomping my way with her raggedy ass sister Cre right behind her. If there was a meme for a "gold diggers" starter pack, her ass would be the picture they used. She was only with Ky because of the little bit of money he was making out here in the streets, and in order to keep it flowing, she'd gotten pregnant within a year of them being together and gave him a son, which he proudly claims.

I tried not to frown at the tight ass maroon and white Pink legging set she wore that looked to be two sizes too small. Her hair looked freshly done in some lemonade braids, and she was rocking the latest Jordan's while Kymia was still wearing the same beat up ass shoes from a few months ago. Her sister was dressed virtually the same except her outfit was black and white, and I couldn't help but feel a small bit of envy. I couldn't even remember the last time I'd been able to set foot inside of Victoria's Secret or buy me anything of high quality. Ever since my boyfriend, Qaud, had gotten locked up three years before, things had been extremely tight for me. He had been like my everything. He made sure the house was straight, and that me and all three of the kids were taken care of. Him getting locked up had been a major blow, but I was no stranger to work, so I jumped right back into it. Three years into a ten-year sentence though, and I was almost at my breaking point.

"Didn't I tell yo' ass the last time you came over here that Ky ain't 'bouta take care of no baby that's not his!" She stated, clapping between each word as she got closer to me. "Ain't that what I said, Cre?"

"Hell yeah!" Her sister co-signed, coming to her side and looking me up and down. I pulled my purse strap higher up on my shoulder and focused my gaze on Pumpkin, making sure to take a deep breath before I spoke.

"You don't got shit to do with what I discuss with Kymere! Especially when it concerns OUR daughter." I made sure to emphasize the *our* part 'cause this bitch was truly delusional if she thought that Kymia didn't belong to him. She looked just like his sorry ass, and we all knew it. I was honestly starting to think they only said that to piss me off.

"Ha! Everything that got to do with MY baby daddy and his money got somethin' to do with me, boo, know that! Everybody knows that yo' ass don't know who that lil girl belong to. KJ is his only kid and it's gone stay that way 'til I give him another one!" She smirked and rubbed her pudgy midsection before continuing. "Yo' ass only comin' around anyway 'cause Quad got knocked!"

"What type of nigga leaves they baby mama out here broke and cleaning up other peoples' cum rags?" Cre asked, crunching up her face.

"A nigga that ain't got no damn money! Shit his ass probably spent his last on them lil drugs. Her ass sholl dress like it!" Pumpkin said, causing them both to erupt into fake laughter. I stood there looking at them both blankly because for one, the shit wasn't even funny and two, I was trying to calm myself down. I wasn't pressed for drama or acting an ass out in public. I'd already just done enough of that with Ky before she got here. Being a mother, I felt that I should carry myself a certain way. The way people were dragging women, especially black women, for everything they did in the media, always made me think before reacting. That was the only thing keeping me from grabbing her ass by them long nappy braids and dragging her around this yard. That and the fact that I didn't have any money to bond out.

"Baby, make this hoe move the fuck around man, over here beggin' and shit!" Ky must have heard her loud mouth ass out here and decided to open the door, adding to the bullshit.

That put the battery right in this bitch's back 'cause she stepped closer and pointed her finger in my face. "You heard him, bitch! Get the fuck on!" She sneered with an evil grin. I gritted back the words that were threatening to come out and explain just how much of my ass, her and her man could kiss. It was already time to pick up my kids from school, and if I spent anymore time out here, I would definitely hit traffic and be late.

With my head held high, I pushed past her and her hefty ass sister, ready to put this entire experience behind me. I had almost made it to my car when I felt a hard push. I tried to catch myself, but all that managed to do was make me fall harder, landing on my wrist. The sharp pain that shot through my arm caused me to yelp while these fools just stood there laughing with their phones out.

I shoved all of my things that had fallen out back into the raggedy Michael Kors purse, ignoring all the eyes I felt on me. My wrist was throbbing, and I just knew that it was sprained, which was going to make working tonight hard as hell. I eased inside my car and prayed that it wouldn't embarrass me further by stalling out here and thankfully, it turned right over. It had been a waste of time and gas money coming over there, but thankfully, mama would come through as always. The check I'd just gotten from my day job was still in my glove box, and even tho' it wasn't much, it would have to be stretched so that I could add shoes to my budget. Letting out a sigh of relief, I pulled away from the curb in the direction of my two youngest kids' school.

SAVAGE

"So, you gon' let me ride with you to the studio, or what? I'm gettin' tired of always actin' like we not like that in public, Ju." This little hoe Kiana that I fucked with whined behind me as I stood in her mirror brushing down my waves. I paused my movements and locked eyes with her without turning around.

"No," I said simply. "And we NOT like that. Me coming over here to fuck is just that, me coming over here to fuck." I squinted my eyes at her to make sure she understood before running the brush over my head a few more times and putting it down into the pocket of my gray Nike shorts. Her beautiful golden colored face balled up, and I knew it was about to be some shit. To avoid the evil glare she was shooting my way, I picked up my vibrating phone from the dresser and let my nigga Troy know that I was on my way before checking my Instagram. I wasn't all that into social media, but if it was a way to escape this conversation, then I was logging in.

I'd been messing with Kiana for the last six months and despite how many times I told her I didn't want a girl, she

6

still pressed. The fact that she was pretty consistent in my rotation occasionally went to her head, and she would try and take things further than I was willing to go. Lately, she hadn't really been causing any problems though. I came and went as I pleased and messed with whoever I wanted without any fuss from her. Me being an up and coming rapper had me keeping fucked up hours, but no matter what time I called she was available, and that led to me being comfortable enough to stay at her crib last night. Something I'd only done maybe three times since we started talking. Usually, I came and got my dick wet then took my ass home, and her ass NEVER stepped foot in my crib. No bitch had, and no bitch would. Me sleeping here had clearly been a mistake 'cause it set us back weeks as far as me wanting to be around her.

If it wasn't for the fact that we had her booked to lay some vocals on a few of our tracks, her ass wouldn't be allowed at the studio either. She stood up from her spot on the bed and stomped over, snatching my phone out my hands and throwing it into the wall, shattering the glass of my iPhone X on impact. I can't lie, that shit pissed me off. Bitches like Kisha always wanted a reaction, but I wasn't even gone give her one. That phone wasn't shit. Besides, I had insurance on it anyway, but she was gone pay for that shit.

"I'm not 'bouta keep playing these games with you, Ju! Why do I have to keep proving to you that I'm the type of bitch you need on your arm? That night at Adrianna's when them niggas started shootin', who got rid of yo' gun for you before 12 showed up? Who gave you an alibi when you and Troy got caught up in that bullshit at the park, huh?" She questioned, snaking her neck so that the long ass weave she was wearing flipped back and forth. I couldn't lie, these past few months, shorty had done all that and more. But, was I supposed to be held responsible for the stupid ass decisions she made for a nigga without any commitment attached?

"Mannnnnn, you did all that shit on yo' own, Kish. I never asked you to do none of that. I'm man enough to take responsibility for my shit 25/8." I told her, walking away and leaving that broke ass phone where it was because I could tell that she was about to turn her ratchet all the way up, and I ain't need that shit before my session. She should have taken that as a cue to leave me the fuck alone, but it just amped her up more 'cause she followed right behind me.

"You man enough for that, but when I ask you to be with me, you're too young tho', right? You can't have it both ways, Ju!" She yelled, mushing my head. I whipped around so fast that she froze up and her eyes widened in surprise. Snatching her by the front of her shirt, I pulled her up until her toes were barely touching the floor.

"Don't. Put. Your. Hands. On. Me." I gritted and shook her little ass with every word. She looked like she was on the verge of tears from a mixture of fear and hurt, but that shit wasn't moving me right now. Honestly, I had never put my hands on Kisha. I never had a reason too, so I'm sure that this was scaring the fuck out of her right now. I sat her back on her feet and ran a hand down my face with a heavy sigh. Maybe it would be best to leave her completely alone for a while 'cause hemming females up wasn't my thing. I'd watched my OG get beat on more than a few times, and I never wanted to be that nigga.

As soon as I let her go, Kisha wrapped her arms around herself and the tears that had been on the brink of falling unleashed and cascaded down her cheeks. This was the emotionally draining shit that made me avoid being with just one woman. I didn't want to be responsible for hurt feelings and keeping a bitch happy. All I wanted to do was get money, make music, and fuck, and not necessarily in that order. I stepped back away from her and closer to the door because I was ready to go.

"My bad, a'ight? I ain't mean to do all that. But I did mean what I said. I'm too young to be tied down to you or anybody else, shit. I'm tryna get this money on the rap tip, and I ain't got time to be worried about nobody else but me." She went to open her mouth, but I cut her smooth off. "You might not understand, but you gone have to respect it." I needed to be as firm with her as possible, so that she would let her hopes of making things official with me rest. Even if she didn't though, I was done fucking with her on a sexual level. I'd still let her make her ends on these mixtapes, but I wasn't putting my dick in her again.

I watched her for a second to make sure her ass didn't follow me again before heading to the door and opening it up. "Yo' ass payin' for my phone too!" I yelled, slamming her door shut behind me, and I walked to my whip.

Besides my condo, my 2017, black on black Camaro was my most prized possession. After I'd moved my OG out the hood, it was the first thing I bought from the profits of my first mixtape. It didn't seem like much to some, but for a twenty-one-year old nigga getting it on his own, I felt like I was doing good for myself. I had put in work on the streets, doing some of anything to help my family out, so I'd gotten the name Savage honest. The hood respected a nigga and my hustle. It wasn't unusual to hear my songs as people drove by or in the clubs. My shit was heat and everybody knew I lived every rhyme I ever spit. Right now, I was shopping around for a label, but still putting out independent shit until I got the right deal. Still, I ain't care how much money I made, I wasn't ever getting rid of this car.

"Heyyyyy, Ju!" Kisha's hoe ass neighbor called out to me from her regular spot on her porch.

She'd been trying to throw the pussy at me since I started

fucking with Kisha, but I didn't fuck with dirty bitches. I ain't never stepped foot in her crib, but I could tell just from looking at her and her dirty ass kids that her house smelled like shitty pampers, 211, and fish. I wouldn't stick dick to her if she had the last pussy on the planet. She looked like she had been hit with every bit of the struggle after having six kids. Today she was wearing some little ass shorts that looked like they were supposed to be white, but were now a grayish color, with a black halter top. Her hair was in a struggling ass ponytail, and whatever gel she'd used was running down her face mixed with sweat. She took a puff of the blunt she was holding and giggled when I threw her a head nod.

"That *Young Hood Savage* go hard," she said, referring to my latest single that had been getting a lot of buzz.

"You already know everything I touch go hard, shorty."

"I bet it do." She flirted back shamelessly as her daughter came over to where she sat and tugged at her leg. Baby girl looked like she was five walking around with a diaper on. I shook my head at the sight of her out there with her hair all over her head and naked besides for the sagging ass diaper she had hanging off her ass.

"You need to put some fuckin clothes on that baby and potty train her big ass instead of sitting out here tryna get some dick." I called out over my shoulder as I made it to my car and climbed in, shutting the door on whatever response her nasty ass was yelling. I made sure to cut the volume all the way up on the instrumental track I had playing and pulled away.

Once I made it to King Dr. where the studio that me and my homie rented each week was, my mood had somewhat lightened, and I had come up with a quick sixteen to the track. The block was crowded as fuck since there was a school at the corner. I wasn't tripping about the few extra minutes that it was gonna take since it was kids running all over and parents stopping their cars in the street. It gave me time to go over my bars, prepare myself for any bullshit Kisha came up there with, and get myself ready to focus. Flipping open the small console in between my seats, I pulled out the prescription bottle I stored there and popped a pill, swallowing it dry. After, I got that down, I lit the half a blunt I put out earlier and inhaled deeply. This shit was my ritual before I ever stepped foot in a booth. For some reason, the effects of the drugs always made me pay close attention to the beats, the background instruments, and speed of my tracks. I changed the song to some slow shit my manager, Mone, kept trying to get me to lay verses to. He said I needed a track for the ladies, but that shit had been hard to come up with. I was a hood nigga and it usually ain't take no sweet talking for me to fuck, so I ain't have no idea what he wanted me to do with this shit. I couldn't lie, the beat was decent, and I found myself bobbing my head to it after the second time it played. The traffic finally started to move to more than just a slow crawl, and I was getting ready to move with it when the impact of somebody hitting the back of my car damn near made my head hit the wheel. I couldn't do shit but close my eyes and try to get a handle on my anger, but it was pointless 'cause my day had just got a whole lot worse and theirs was about to too.

NIVEA

"*This* day can't get no fuckin' worse!" I hissed under my breath, but of course the bionic eared children in my backseat heard me loud and clear.

"Ooooh, mama said a curse word!" My middle child Quiana giggled.

"Ooooh," Quad Jr. repeated, covering up his mouth. I shot them both a look and they quieted down. They had already been working my nerves and had only been in the car five minutes. Now I'd ran into somebody trying to referee them from the front seat. I cringed at the damage on the car in front of me. This was the very last thing that I needed today, or any other day for that matter. My insurance had literally just lapsed a month ago, and I was filled with dread at what my car might look like considering the way that their trunk was balled up. I put the gear in reverse and the sound of metal scraping against metal filled the air and caused the kids to shriek.

"Be quiet, y'all!" I shouted this time. My heart was pounding hard as hell, and I honestly contemplated running, but before I could talk myself into it, one of the finest nigga's

I'd ever seen stepped out with a deep scowl on his face and a blunt dangling from his lips. He stomped his way to the rear of his car and looked over the damage making the frown deepen.

"Get yo' ass out, shorty!" He barked, glaring my way. I could see him mumbling to himself as he continued to look between the cars. I took my time shutting off my car and unhooking my seat belt because I didn't know what he was capable of. Nigga's these days were killing people for less and the last thing I wanted was for me and my kids to end up on the news.

"I'm locking the doors, Quiana. Stay y'all asses in your seats and in this car. Don't open the door for nothin'," I coached her as I opened the door.

"But Ma-"

"Just do what I said!" I told her, shutting the door on any further protests she might have had. My legs felt like jello as soon as I stood on them and started walking the short distance to where he was standing in between our cars. The moment I hit the locks, he looked at me and sucked his teeth, but I didn't give a fuck. My kid's safety was everything to me and I didn't know his ass from Adam. He blew a thick cloud of smoke my way, and I used my good hand to wave it out of my face.

"You know this shit yo' fault, right?"

I nodded my head as I looked at both cars and tried to mentally calculate how much it would be to repair both. It didn't take me but a second to realize that it would be well over a thousand dollars. A thousand dollars that I didn't have. The back end of his car was bent all the way up and his trunk was literally in his backseat. I could see speckles of white paint from my car in a few spots and my front end was dented with the bumper hanging on the ground.

"Aye! You heard what the fuck I said?!" He snapped,

bringing my attention back to him. His expression didn't seem any less angry as he peered down at me, but that didn't take away from his looks. His light complexioned skin was unblemished and smooth despite the wrinkles that had appeared in his forehead displaying his annoyance. The thin mustache and chin hair he had gave away that he was years younger than me. I tried not to show how nervous I was as I gazed up at him.

"Bring me yo' insurance! I ain't got time to just be standin' here!" His voice boomed, causing me to jump back a little. He was clearly big mad, and I could understand that, but after the day I had, I wasn't feeling another soul coming at me crazy.

"Listen, you don't gotta be yellin' and cussin' at me, okay? I'll go get my information for you, but you need to be getting yours too... if yo' ass even got insurance." I grumbled that last part and headed back towards my car, talking shit the whole way. His young ass barely looked old enough to have insurance and if he did, it was probably in his baby mama name.

People had already started to gather on the sidewalk being nosy. Some had their phones out and others were just watching, either waiting for a fight to break out or commentating on how badly both our cars looked. Other drivers were blowing their horns and yelling shit, but I just waved for them to go around in frustration. I was ready to throw the whole day away already, and I hadn't even picked up Ky's cranky ass. When I made it back to my car, Quiana was sitting in the front seat messing with my phone and Quad was struggling to climb out of his car seat with a face full of tears. I cursed under my breath and unlocked the doors, surprising them both.

"Quiana, didn't I tell you not to move? You're watching those damn videos and yo' brother back there crying!" I snatched my phone out of her hand and gave Quad the sippy cup filled with apple juice out of the cup holder that I'm sure he had been reaching for. He hungrily grabbed ahold of it and sat back guzzling it down while I pretended to look for my "insurance card".

"Mama, I'm hungry," was her only response. I figured she was. They were always hungry after school and whenever we weren't around any food.

Sighing for what felt like the millionth time today, I snapped the glovebox closed after making a show of leaning over to look into it and started searching through my middle console for a pen and paper. I had an idea and hopefully it would get me out of having to pay for anything but my own damage. "I know baby, just give me a few more minutes, ok?" With the paper in hand I dialed up my best friend, Saniyah, hoping that she wasn't busy or sleeping for work tonight.

"What's up bitch!" She answered loudly. I said a silent thank you to the man upstairs and quickly filled her in on what had happened. Thankfully, she said she was nearby and could be here in less than fifteen minutes.

By the time I was finished talking to her, the guy was already walking my way. Instead of letting him get too close, I just got out and met him halfway with a forced attitude of my own, even though I was honestly scared shitless. "I can't find my card, but I can give you my name and number, and your insurance company can bill mine," I said, sucking my teeth and planting my hand on my hip. I watched as his brows knitted together while he tried to figure out if he should trust my word or not.

"Man, gone head and write that shit down," he huffed dismissively. "That shit better not be fake neither." I could tell he didn't really want to let it go, but what choice did he have? If he was smart, he would have demanded that I put down my license plate number too or maybe even my driver's license number, but he didn't ask for either and I wasn't about to hand it over anyway. The first name that came to mind was Lakisha Smith, so that's what I wrote down along with a random ass house phone number. I could feel him watching me intensely, but I managed to keep my cool. Handing over the paper, I waited while he looked it over and held my breath.

"Lakisha Smith, huh? Yo' ass ain't got no cell, just a house phone?" He questioned, and I gave him a half-hearted shrug. I'm sure he wanted to ask more questions, but I stopped him by asking one of my own.

"Don't you need to be giving me your information too?"

"This shit wasn't my fault. You don't need shit from me but a bill, bitch!" The small bit of resolve I'd been trying to hold on to, disappeared the minute this nigga called me out my name. After all the bullshit I had dealt with today and kept cool, something inside of me snapped.

"Bitch!? You know what, nigga, fuck you! Yeah, I said it! All I asked yo' lil bum ass for was your insurance and I gotta be a Bitch?" I let out a maniacal laugh as his eyes widened in shock. "Yeah, fuck you! Fuck yo' car! And fuck yo' insurance!"

I didn't even wait for him to respond before turning around so that I could get to my damn kids, but thankfully, Saniyah pulled up right then. When I turned around, he was still standing there looking confused and that's just what his ass got. Granted I had given him a fake name and number, and I really didn't need his insurance because the accident was my fault, but besides that, I had been pretty cooperative with him. I didn't deserve to be called a bitch though. I grabbed QJ out of the car and motioned for Quiana to come on too. Saniyah said she had already called me a tow truck, so I was good to go.

"Biiitch! Do you know who that is?" She asked me as we drove past the guy still standing in the street next to his car.

"Nope, and I don't care either. Fuck his lil rude ass." Before Quiana could say anything about me cursing, I whipped around and shook my head at her. I was not in the mood.

"Well, I'ma tell you anyway, with yo' lame ass. That's Ju Savage," she said, glancing between me and the street. When I still didn't say anything, she frowned and sucked her teeth. "You really need to get out more for real. He's got that song *Young Hood Savage*. I know yo' ass done heard it before?"

I shook my head 'cause I hadn't heard of him or that damn song, but just by the name alone, I knew it wasn't my type of music. Saniyah gave me a look filled with pity, but what could I do? I was barely ever able to go out and if I did happen to get a sitter, I was usually too tired to even go anywhere and ended up just falling asleep. It wasn't intentional, but between working two jobs, the kids, stress, and Quad, I barely had time for myself, let alone time to go and spend money.

"So, he's a rapper?"

"Bitch, he's THE rapper! He's like Lil Durk, Gherbo, and Bibby all wrapped up in one. Mmmm!" She moaned and bit her lip as I looked at her with my nose wrinkled.

"Am I supposed to know any of them dumb ass names you just dropped?" I went through my mental rolodex of all the times I'd heard Quad listening to the bullshit ass songs he liked and still came up with a blank. My taste in music had always been nineties based and just about anything RnB. Kymia still liked all that hood trap shit, but when she had her music playing, I wasn't listening to that shit.

"Girl, you need a life for real." Saniyah tsk'ed with the same look of pity as before. "Why don't you come out with me and my girls one of these weekends? I only ever get to see you at work or with these kids. Live a little. Hell, you're only twenty-nine and you act like you fifty." She continued once we pulled up to Kymia's school.

"That's because I have responsibilities, Niyah. I can't just pick up and go out. I gotta get a sitter and make sure I have money to blow. Plus, do you know how they whine whenever I do try to leave them?" I asked with a frown.

Quad Jr. would start crying as soon as I even looked like I was about to leave, Quiana was a bug, and Kymia had too much attitude. The only person I even knew to ask was my mama, and she didn't play that shit. Just the thought of struggling to get her to babysit while I went anywhere gave me a headache. Roberta Hynes didn't babysit nobody's kids for free, and sometimes even when I paid her, I still had to hear her mouth. She felt like she'd done her job raising me and my little sister Nadia and right now, she was trying to live her best life. At fifty-years old, she didn't look a day over thirty-five, and had spent the last twelve years traveling and enjoying what she called her "freedom".

"I know people with four and five kids that go out more than you, and that's a whole lot of responsibility, but they still make time for themselves. Like my cousin, Kisha. She got two lil girls and her ass ALWAYS out."

"Do she take good care of them, tho'? Spend time with them? Provide? Cause if she ALWAYS out, then I don't see how she doin' any of that." I shot out question after question.

"Now that you mention it, I think she did lose custody of them to her baby daddy," she admitted sheepishly. "She's not a good example, but-"

"See, I ain't fuckin' with you girl." I held up my hand, cutting her off as I watched Kymia strut away from the bus stop with an evil expression. It was obvious she had an attitude as usual, but she knew better than to try and get her grown ass on the bus.

"Move!" She snapped at Quiana when she finally made it over to us huffing and puffing while she got in and slammed the door shut behind her.

"Ky, watch that attitude. She ain't do nothin' to you! And ain't no damn body tell you to try and ride the bus neither!" I turned around to face her so that she could see the seriousness on my face.

"You the one who was late and since my phone not on again, I couldn't even call you." She smacked her lips and if it wasn't for my hand being sore, I would have smacked them right off her damn face.

"I was in an accident. Didn't you notice that Saniyah, who you haven't even spoken to, is giving us a ride? And as far as your phone, it's gonna stay off if you don't get yo' mouth and attitude under control," I told her, facing the front of the car again. "Now speak to Niyah, with yo' rude ass."

"Hey, Saniyah," she grumbled.

"Hello to you too, Ky," Saniyah said cheerfully like only someone without a teenager could. If she was feeling any type of way about the conversation, I couldn't tell, but I knew she was probably shocked. Little did she know, this was just a day in the life for me. It was a welcome distraction when she finally cut the radio back up to fill the silence that had taken over the car.

SAVAGE

*H*ours later and shorty from the accident was still on my mind. Maybe it was because she gave me a fake name and number, so she wouldn't have to pay for my shit. Or maybe it was because as hard as I tried to be mad at her, I couldn't. She had that understated beauty that was often passed up by niggas like me. Bitches these days were drawing their eyebrows on and creating whole new faces with makeup just to be video vixens. And niggas was eating that shit up. I was guilty of it too. Only letting "Bad bitches" in my presence. But shorty was different, I could tell. As soon as she stepped out of her beat up ass Impala, I forgot what I was even mad about. She wasn't like any of these hoes out here that would have been flirting as soon as she saw me. In fact, I don't even think she knew who I was, and that shit was rare for me. Not trying to sound conceited or nothing, but since before I even stepped into this music shit, bitches had been on my dick. So, you can imagine how much more atten-tion I got now. Even at the accident, people were out there screaming my name and recording and shit, but she didn't even notice 'cause she was so scared. I chuckled as I thought about her trying to get all jazzy and shit once her friend pulled up. I should have known she was on bullshit then, having someone pick her up even though she claimed she ain't have a cell.

"Nigga, did you finish that verse you was workin' on while you over there day dreamin'?" Troy asked, looking up from the notepad he was holding. We had finished the two songs that we came in to record and were now working on our verses for a feature. It was a rap group out here named The Goon Squad, and they had reached out to Mone for us to be on their new song. They had a nice little buzz building, so I agreed. Word on the street was that they would be the Chicago version of the Migos, except they were all still heavy in the streets. Which kind made me feel the need to be cautious whenever they were around. Like right now, I had my Ruger sitting comfortably on my lap just in case something popped off while them niggas was here. I'd even went so far as to make Kisha's bug ass go home earlier after she finished her recording instead of sitting around here like she normally did. The whole time she was there, all she did was stare all in my face anyway and make a big deal out of stupid shit to get my attention. She had even dressed a little bit sexier than she usually did. The sundress she had on had her breasts and ass sitting right, and I knew damn well she ain't even have a bra on. Probably didn't have on panties either. Little did she know that while that may have gotten me to look once or twice, it wasn't enticing enough to make me change my mind. I wasn't fucking with her ass period.

Even seeing that I wasn't entertaining her bullshit, she still kept up with her antics. Troy stupid ass just watched in amusement the whole time, not saying shit while I tried to avoid even having to look at her. When her ass tried to lean across the board and start asking questions about it was when I knew I needed to move around. I took that as my opportunity to go and call shorty, figuring that she should have been home by then and taken whoever kids she was babysitting home too. She didn't look old enough to have a kid as old as the big one, so I naturally assumed they didn't belong to her. I didn't even realize she had kids in the car until she pulled them out when her ride came. That must have been why she'd locked the doors when she got out.

When some lady answered and said that it was taco bell I had called, I couldn't do shit but laugh. Her ass had straight played me. It didn't matter, my insurance would pay it regardless, but it was still fucked up on her part. Especially since I knew now that I wouldn't get the chance to see her again since I didn't even know her name.

"Damn, man. Let me find out yo' ass still thinkin' 'bout that shit from earlier," Troy said once I still hadn't answered him. "That shit gone get fixed."

"I ain't even trippin' off that," I scoffed. He looked at me for a long time before his face split into a wide grin, and he started nodding his head.

"Ohhhh, you thinkin' 'bout ole girl playin' yo' ass!"

I don't know how he figured that. I'd only brought up her sending me off one time and that was a minute ago, right after I had called the number. This nigga had always been over-intuitive when it came to me and my inner thoughts though. Ever since we were kids, he knew if something was bothering me.

I waved his ass off, still in denial about wanting to talk to her. "Man, ain't nobody thinkin' 'bout that bitch." That shit sounded good, but he saw right through it.

"Yo' ass flodgin', nigga, you know you wanna find her. And I know it ain't just cause of the car either." He spoke like he was speaking straight facts, and he was.

At first, I was insistent on her paying for the damage, but after sitting here, I realized that I just wanted to see her again. I could tell by how she carried herself that she was different from the type of girls I was used to dealing with, like she was mature in a way that they wouldn't be for years. *Damn! I'm seriously sitting here thinkin' 'bout her hard!* I realized. That shit was crazy, and something that I had never done. Still, I didn't want to admit it to Troy's worrisome ass.

Thankfully, I didn't have to because right then, The Goon Squad shuffled in with an entourage of like ten other niggas and two bitches that looked like strippers. Without meaning too, I laughed as soon as I laid eyes on these niggas. They may have claimed to be hood, but I hadn't ever met no thug that was on the block in some skinny jeans. I shared a look with Troy who could barely contain himself. I guess neither of us had done much research on them.

"What's up man," I said, dapping up the first one that had walked in. His eyes dropped to my piece still sitting out openly on my lap, but he didn't say shit as he greeted me. "Y'all cool and all, but them other niggas and them hoes gotta go, man." Immediately, all chatter stopped, and everyone's eyes landed on me. The fact that it was so many of them didn't move me one way or another. Like I said, I lived this shit, so no man put fear in me, especially one that was wearing female type jeans.

"Nigga, what you say?" The toughest one out of them asked, pushing the girl he was hugged up with off him and taking a step in my direction. His girl started grumbling about a ride while dude stared me down.

"Nigga, I said y'all gotta ride. I don't like all that kickin' it shit during a session." I let him know, unmoved by his antics.

"I ain't gotta go no fuckin' where. I'm their manager and this is their security. I'm the one that set this whole shit up with Mone in the first place!" He puffed out his chest like he was intimidating somebody. True, he may have been a little bit more stocky than me, but that would only slow his big ass down. Of course, looking at my light skin ass, he probably thought I was cotton soft. Most niggas did until I made them respect my g.

I lifted my gun from my lap but held it down at my side as I stood to my feet. Troy did the same. My boy already knew if one jumped, we all do. Dude followed the movement with his eyes and frowned harder like he wasn't fazed, but the bravest nigga don't gotta be scared to get shot. The people behind him looked uneasy like they were unsure of what to do, and so did The Goon Squad.

"I'ma let that slick shit slide 'cause you might not know about me, but I don't give a fuck who you are or what you set up with Mone. You see that nigga ain't here, right? He knows ain't nobody in the studio but artists. Whether he relayed that message to you or not ain't my problem. I'm tellin' you that you gotta bounce." He went to say something else but goon number one stopped him.

"Be easy, Jay," he warned, grabbing his arm. "Just go, man. We gone cut this track, then meet back up wit' y'all later."

The nigga Jay looked down at the arm ole dude's hand was on and then back up at him before eyeballing me. I flashed his mad ass a grin, not giving a single fuck. This song wasn't shit that I needed to do so it was whatever for me. Finally, deciding to listen to his boy, he snatched the keys that he was holding out to him and waved for the rest of them niggas to follow him.

"Let's roll man!" He snorted, walking out of the room without waiting for them to follow. Once the last of them left, leaving only the skinny jean crew, goon number one gave me an apologetic look.

"Aye man, I'm sorry 'bout that shit y'all. If we woulda known, we wouldn't have brung them niggas with us, real shit."

"It's cool," I dismissed, my mood simmering down now

that the cause of my irritation was gone. "Let's just gone head and lay this track."

"Man, yo' ass a bug, nigga." Troy laughed and shook his head while I shrugged. "I'm Trigga, and this fool is Ju." He introduced us to the trio, and we all bumped fists.

"I'm Keys, this my brother Kb, and that's our boy G." The one who'd apologized went down the line.

"Ok, ok, that's what's up."

"Where y'all niggas from?" Troy asked as he sat back down. His ass was always tryna be friendly. I wasn't tryna sit here and listen to their life story, and I hoped he wasn't planning on that shit either.

"Southside all day." Keys boasted with a lazy grin. Troy and I nodded 'cause that was our side of town too.

"Right, right, but look, let's gone get this shit over with," I said, finally taking a seat and putting my gun back on my lap.

"You gone leave that shit out the whole time?" Kb finally spoke, dropping his eyes down to the gun.

"Yeah, it helps me think," I told him, causing Troy's silly ass to snicker. Keys and G joined in, but little did they know, I was dead ass serious. Kb seemed to be the only one who understood that I wasn't playing judging from how he kept eyeing me.

Eventually, we got to work letting them record their verses first since me and Troy were coming in at the end of the song anyway. I knew that shit was gone be a hit as soon as the beat dropped, and Keys hit the mic. I'd heard a few of their songs before deciding to actually work with them, but they were eating on this beat. It went way harder than any of the shit I had heard from them. I guess having me and Troy on this joint had them going in. I leaned all the way back in the chair and bobbed my head.

"They eatin' on this shit, right?" Troy asked, nodding his head to the beat too with a big ass grin.

"Hell yeah." I agreed, getting amped up. I couldn't wait to lay my verse down after hearing Kb, Keys, and G in the booth. "That shit was lit as fuck," I told them casually when they came out.

"On baby." Troy co-signed, slapping hands with G who was the last one out and standing the closest to him. They all grinned widely at the compliment coming from us.

"So, who's next?" G asked, rubbing his hands together as he looked between me and Troy. As bad as I wanted to go and finish this shit, the excitement on my homie's face told me to let him go first. The nigga legit looked like he was about to jump out his seat.

"Gone head, man," I said, gesturing for him to go inside the booth. He hopped up so fast, the chair he was sitting in was still spinning. I just shook my head at his ass and started the track back up, cueing him in. He started off talking shit about this rapper from Detroit that had been running his mouth about us named Stacks. For damn near two minutes, the homie did his thing, and then came out with the cockiest smirk on his face as the Goon Squad bigged him up.

"You know I just killed that shit, right?" He bragged, plopping back down next to me. This nigga stayed talking shit but called me a bug.

"You got that, lil nigga, but watch me work tho'." I nodded, giving him props, and slapping hands with him before I headed in. I wasn't like Troy's ass though. Talking shit on the mic wasn't my thing, especially when it came to that bitch ass nigga Stacks. He wasn't gone get no shine off me.

Almost two hours later, we had perfected the track and were finishing up a celebratory smoke session. My little ass was high and sleepy as fuck when I finally stood to leave. Usually I was the first nigga talking about hitting up the club or IHOP or some shit, but after the day I had, I could barely keep my eyes open. I know my OG was probably pissed the fuck off that she couldn't reach me today, but after the accident, I didn't really have no time to go out and get another phone. I'd have to just wait until in the morning and hope she ain't spazz on me too hard.

"Damn nigga, you ready to leave this early?" Troy questioned, raising his eyebrows in shock.

"Hell yeah! We been at this shit for hours, it's late, and I'm tired as hell."

"It's late?" He repeated, looking even more surprised by my words. His ass called himself being funny 'cause he knew I never really went in early, but I was really beat. Dealing with Kisha and then getting in a car accident with shorty had me drained all of a sudden. That was two stressors too many and a nigga like me wasn't used to dealing with stress like that.

I stuffed my gun into the waistband of my shorts and nodded. "Hell yeah, it's late! Quit tryna be funny and shit and come drop me off."

"Don't take that shit out on me, bro. You the one letting these hoes stress you. Yo' ass better start treatin' these bitches like I be doin'," he lectured, gathering all of his stuff and throwing it inside the backpack he always brought.

"This ain't got shit to do with them," I lied.

"Yeah, a'ight! Kisha ass was in here doin' the most earlier, and you were barely payin' her ass any attention, so I know she did somethin' to piss you off," he pried, falling into step beside me as we exited the room. I realized that I hadn't gotten a chance to tell him about what happened at her crib that day and quickly filled him in while we walked past Pree's office. "Damnnn, her ass broke yo' phone? I woulda broke her shit too, nigga. You better than me."

"Fuck her! Bitch was tryna get a reaction outta me, and I

ain't have shit for her, but she better run me my money for that shit," I muttered, getting irritated all over again.

"Aye Pree!" Troy stopped by the office door and called out to the older man. "We out!" He let him know. Pree just nodded and stuck his head back down into the papers he was looking over. He had always been short with his words. Even when he'd come into the studio to check out what we were working on, he never said much. I'd heard he was an OG, but I never got that vibe from him, and just figured he was an old head that liked music.

"Yeah, well I woulda took my stack up outta her shit." He jumped right back into the conversation we were having. "I play about a lot of things, but I don't play about my phone."

"Nah, it ain't that serious. You, Pree, Mone and my OG the only people I really call anyway, 'cause Jadiyah too little to have a damn phone," I argued, referring to my little sister.

About eight years before, my mama must have been going through a crisis 'cause she went and got pregnant with her. She never said who it was by, but I'm assuming we shared the same deadbeat since we looked so much alike down to our complexion and the dimples. My OG was the complete opposite of us, being the most perfect shade of mahogany that I'd ever seen without a dimple in sight. She never really talked bad about our "father". She just never brought him up, and I never asked. Seeing her struggle made me not even want to know, but she had told me that Jadiyah was starting to wonder. That had me ready to find his ass and force him to bring his sorry self around just for her. I loved my little sister and would do anything for her, even face a nigga I never wanted to make contact with.

"Like I said, you a better man than me," Troy scoffed and pushed open the doors for us to walk out into the stale night air.

I decided not to keep going back and forth with him

'cause we both felt different ways about the situation. Remaining silent as we started towards his silver jeep, I paused and looked around. Some shit just didn't feel right. I grabbed Troy by the arm to stop him, listening at how quiet it was besides the soft purring of a car nearby. Before either of us could reach for our guns, a black Monte Carlo that was parked two cars down from Troy's cut its lights on.

"You ain't the only one with guns, pussy!" Was all I heard and then a chorus of shots rang out. I ducked down by the side of the dumpster in front of the building. By the time I pulled my gun out to shoot back, I wasn't hitting shit but the back end of the car because they were screeching away.

"Troy! Troy!" I called out and panic set in when I saw him lying on the ground by his car door with a bullet hole gushing blood from his chest. "Fuck!"

"Nigga, what you standing there screaming for? Take me to the damn hospital," he moaned out in pain before passing out.

NIVEA

"*D*amn bitch! I wished you woulda called me sooner, 'cause I been waiting to put my hands on that bitch Pumpkin!" Saniyah fumed and bounced her leg rapidly underneath the nurses' station.

"Girl, shhhhhh." I scolded her loud ass. I'd been telling her about what had happened today before I got in the accident since I didn't get a chance to earlier, and I could tell she was pissed. She knew of Ky before she met me and claimed to have never liked him. Apparently, the horror stories I had told her made it worse.

"Tuh! These damn people can't hear me as loud as they got the tv's in this bitch. I'd swear they asses only came to the hospital for the cable." She sucked her teeth in irritation and waved me off.

We worked third shift together in the emergency room at Jackson Park Hospital. Most nights it did seem like people only came in to watch tv 'cause they were coming in and bringing their kids for shit that wasn't even close to emergencies. Like the lady who I'd just taken into a room had brought her son in because he had cut his finger. The shit wasn't even that deep, and I had to stop myself from telling her to take him home and put a band-aid on that it, but I needed my job. There were times that we got serious cases like gun shots and stab victims. Shit, this was Chicago, but it wasn't as often as people liked to think.

"Yo' ass a fool," I said, shaking my head.

"Naw, they some damn fools, comin' in here and taking beds from real sick people just to watch tv," she grumbled and looked at her phone as it dinged with a notification. Her face blossomed into a huge smile, and she hurried to return the message to whoever it was.

"Awww shit, let me find out you got a new boo," I teased, nudging her with my arm.

Saniyah seemed to be living the life while I stood on the sidelines and watched. Damn near everyday she came in with a new story about a nigga she met or club she went to. She had a ton of pictures of her traveling to all of these cool places with her friends. And the shopping trips. She literally had me drooling most times at the cute clothes she could afford to buy herself since she had no obligations besides herself. I found myself living vicariously through her often and wishing that things could be different for me.

Don't get me wrong, I loved my kids. It was just that I wished I had made better decisions for my life and then maybe I wouldn't be struggling so hard. Almost every day was hard for me. I often felt like I failed myself and in turn failed them every time I had to explain to one of them that I couldn't afford something. Every time we couldn't go nice places, to see the sad looks on their faces broke my heart. Which is why I was working hard to finish my Associates of Arts while working two jobs. Reading had always been something that I loved to do and often, without trying to, I would correct common mistakes and fix sentences in things that I read. I figured if doing that came so naturally and reading was my passion, it would make perfect sense to be an editor. The pay was also good which would allow us to live comfortably. I was already a year in and still had one more to go before I would be graduating, and I damn sure couldn't wait. The next step would be opening up my own publishing company.

"Girl, that's just this dude Chase I met when we went to the boat last weekend." She gushed with a smile. I wondered briefly what it would be like to be reckless with money and go gamble. My money was way too damn funny for anything like that though.

"Okayyyy and? I need details. What he look like? Have y'all been on a date?" I wanted to know, pushing the textbook that I'd just been reading away.

"Wellll, he walked up to me while I was playing the slots and said that a woman as gorgeous as me shouldn't be playing no cheap ass slots. I should have a nigga bankrolling me at one of the tables. So, you know me, I went right with his ass to the black jack table. He pulled out this big ass roll of money and handed it to me!" She shrieked, showing me with her hands how big it was. My eyes widened, and I leaned in closer, amazed. "Well, he basically sat next to me and told me what to play so I could win. Swear to God I walked outta there with double what he gave me."

I'm sure when she finished her story, my mouth was hanging wide open. I remembered how Quad used to give me handfuls of money just because. It had been so long since I'd held a whole bunch of money in my hands that I probably would pass out if it ever happened again. "He was fine as hell too, girl. Tall, dark skinned with dreads. Lawd, you know dreads is my weakness!" She continued, throwing her head back and closing her eyes.

I couldn't do shit but laugh at her over dramatic ass, acting like she was passed out until I saw our supervisor,

Nurse Sherice, heading our way. I hurried and tapped Niyah's arm, so she could get back to work. "Here come Sherice, bitch." I warned and sat one of the charting books in front of me like I'd been writing in it the whole time. Saniyah did the same thing except she smacked her lips and rolled her eyes so hard, I thought one of the long ass lashes she wore would get caught up in them.

"Ain't nobody worried 'bout her stiff ass," she griped. "The bitch need to get some dick and she wouldn't have so much time on her hands."

"But I see you doin' that damn charting tho.'"

"I see yo' ass is too." Saniyah noted with a raised brow, and I stuck my tongue out at her.

Surprising us both, Sherice just hurried past us and out of the double doors that led to the emergency room entrance. We shared a look as another round of nurses and a doctor rounded the same corner and exited where Sherice had.

"Where the hell they goin'?"

Saniyah took the words right out of my mouth. All night it had been pretty quiet and we hadn't had anybody come in by ambulance, so it must have been serious whatever they were running to. It didn't take us long to find out when they all ran right back in with the patient on a stretcher. They rushed past us with a man covered in blood running behind them. He even tried to follow them into the back but Sherice stopped him. They were too far away for me to hear what she was saying, but I was pretty sure it was that he couldn't come into the back. I could tell that wasn't what he wanted to hear by the way his fists clenched, and his back flexed underneath the t-shirt he wore. The sound of someone's call light buzzing drew my attention to the wall where the room numbers were located.

"That's you, bitch." Saniyah's nosy ass said without looking away from the dramatic scene in front of her.

"How the hell you know?" I asked with a hand on my hip.

"Cause yo' lights sound different from mine." She shrugged still looking down the hall. I sucked my teeth and mumbled bitch under my breath as I walked off to see what my patient wanted.

"You rang?" I asked as cheerfully as I could once I made it to the room that Ms. Price was in with her five-year old daughter. The look she gave me let me know that she was about to start some shit.

"Yeah, I rang! We been in here for over three hours waiting on the results to her blood work. I wanna know what's taking so fuckin' long!" She snarled with her hands on her hips.

"Well, ma'am, I'm not sure what is taking the results so long, but I'll be more than happy to go and ask for you," I offered, trying to remain calm. This wasn't the worst situation I had been in while working here, and I always managed to walk away with my job intact.

"Nah uh! Nope! Yo' ass say you gone find out, but all you gone do is go sit yo' ass right back down behind the nurses' station! Go find me somebody who got some news for me right now! If it ain't a doctor in here in the next five minutes, I'ma tear this bitch up!" She threatened, taking a step closer to me. When shit like this happened, I took three deep breaths, and repeated my kids' names to remind me of what I do this for. If it wasn't for them, I would have been fired or quit this job twenty times already.

"Ok, I'll go get someone right away," I said, backing up until I reached the door and hurrying out of the room. I didn't miss her calling me a stupid bitch when she thought I was too far away to hear. It took three hail Mary's, a prayer, and recalling how many hours of labor it took to have ALL my kids to stop me from turning around.

When I made it back to the nurses' station, Saniyah's ass

was still sitting there and must have saw the irritation in my face.

"Damn, what happened that fast?" She questioned with a frown. I gave her a quick rundown before paging the doctor for that room. "I swear you be getting all the extra people."

"Tell me about it," I grumbled, looking at the time. I had no doubt that Ms. Price would come out acting a damn fool like she'd threatened if she didn't talk to somebody and soon. When the doctor still hadn't brought his ass down or answered my page, I decided to just call the lab and find out for myself what was the hold up. Whoever answered gave me the run around, and I was just about to lose the last little bit of restraint I had when I spotted Ms. Price storming my way.

"Oh shit," Saniyah mumbled under her breath.

"See, I knew yo' ass was gone come and sit right back down! Didn't I tell you five minutes!" She yelled as she came up the hall.

"Ma'am, I-"

"I don't wanna hear shit! I wanna talk to yo' supervisor right muthafuckin' now! Right now!" She interrupted, banging a fist on the nurses' station with every word. I could feel the small bit of professionalism I had fading the more she talked and knew it was only a matter of time before I said fuck her and this job.

"Girrrrrrl," I heard Saniyah say, obviously getting irritated with the lady just like me. She had managed to draw the attention of everyone that was out in the halls and they all watched, being nosy to see if some shit was about to kick off. It didn't take long for Sherice to come out and approach us, looking at me like it was my fault before she even knew what happened.

"What seems to be the problem, ma'am?" She asked Ms. Price and completely ignored me. I shared a look with Saniyah because we both knew how this shit went. Anytime

Sherice received a complaint about either of us, we automatically got a write up whether we were right or wrong. So far, since she'd begun working here, she had written me up five times and she hadn't even been here a year!

"Yes, me and my daughter been sittin' in here for three hours because she had a temp over 103, and they wanted to do blood work, but not one soul has been back since they took her damn blood!" She paused, and they both looked at me like that shit was my fault. She stared me down as she continued. "I came out numerous times and saw her ass just sitting here not doin' shit!"

"Actually, Ms. Price, I-"

"Let her finish, Nivea." Sherice cut me off and raised her hand to silence me. Ms. Price smirked evilly and then went right back to telling the story with even more made up shit.

"Like I was sayin'!" She spat, rolling her eyes. "I pushed the call light and waited damn near thirty minutes before she finally came in actin' like she had an attitude!"

"Now wait a minute, you know damn well it ain't take me that long, and you the one who had the attitude!" I finally said, unable to take the bullshit anymore. She leaned back and clutched her imaginary pearls like she hadn't just been over here acting a damn fool.

"See! You see what I'm talkin' 'bout? She doesn't need to be workin' with people with a nasty ass attitude like that!" She shrieked, pointing across the desk at me.

"Bitch, I'ma show you a nasty attitude!"

"Nivea! I think you need to go on home for the night!" Sherice dismissed.

"She needs to be fired! I can't believe y'all be hiring people like this! She shouldn't be around people who can't defend themself!" She continued her rant.

"Now, Sherice, you know she's lyin'," Saniyah finally said. "Nivea is never rude when she deals with patients and you know that." She tried to reason with our supervisor, but from the look on Sherice's face, she wasn't trying to hear shit either one of us had to say.

"Oh, maybe you need to be sent home too," Sherice threatened.

"Baby, you ain't said nothin' but a word." Saniyah started packing up the things she had on the desk. "I'll go home right now, rest my feet and binge watch Scandal, shiiit."

Suddenly, Sherice didn't seem as tough, and she started stuttering.

"No, no, you stay, Saniyah. We still need someone on the floor, but you..." She flicked her eyes my way and turned her nose up. "You need to leave, and we can discuss whether or not you still have a job tomorrow."

"Oh, hell naw." Saniyah dropped her bag, ready to go off.

"Naw, it's cool Niyah. I don't want you gettin' in trouble for me." I stopped her from saying anything else. There was no need to try and argue my point. Sherice had been itching to fire me since she started here and the last thing I wanted was for Saniyah to lose her job too.

"You 'bouta let the only other good aide up in here leave over some false allegations," she fussed as I packed away my school book and the notes I'd taken.

"She ain't the only aide in Chicago. This hospital was running just fine before her and it would probably be even better when she leaves," Ms. Price answered for Sherice, but I'm sure she was thinking the same thing.

The whole time I got my shit to leave, I was already thinking of other hospitals or nursing homes that I could apply to. I still had my part time job to hold me over; things would just be tighter than usual.

"Don't you got a sick daughter you need to be worried 'bout while you out here causing all this trouble?" Saniyah questioned.

"Don't you have work to do?" She countered, twisting her lips up in irritation.

"Girl, you got the right one messin' with me-"

"Niyah, I said it's cool. I'll talk to you later, ok." I urged, holding on to her arm until she nodded and said ok. I slung my backpack over my shoulder and walked around the desk with my head held high even though I felt like breaking down in tears. Just as I got to the double doors though, I turned around to see Sherice and Ms. Price still standing there staring after me. The same feeling of anger from earlier took over, and I started right back in their direction.

"You know what, fuck you and this job, Sherice. You done had it out for me since you got here, and I still came in and treated you and every patient that walked through the door with respect. I don't need this shit. There are plenty other places that will hire me and probably pay way more! So good luck finding somebody else to replace me and you!" I glared at Ms. Price. "You're an evil old bitch. I don't know who you mad at, but you came here and took it out on me. You better hope I don't ever see you outside this hospital, or I'ma beat yo' ass!"

"Oh, you definitely don't need to come back after that!" Sherice called out after me. I didn't even give her the satisfaction of facing her. I just threw up the peace sign as I pushed open the double doors.

"I don't plan on it, bitch!" I heard a slow clap and knew it was Saniyah's crazy ass. I could bet the last five dollars in my pocket that she would be calling me before I could even make it to the bus stop. Even though I'd just lost my primary source of income, I felt like a weight had been lifted off my shoulders, and I couldn't help but smile as I exited the sliding glass doors. Well, until I heard a voice that made me freeze right up.

"I'ma need that real name and number up outcha."

SAVAGE

Shorty looked like she had seen a ghost when she stepped outside. I'm sure I was the last person she wanted to see after the shit that had just went down in there. The way ole girl was going off had to have her heated. Honestly, I admired the way she kept it together 'cause I know it was killing her to keep quiet. At the same time, I was happy when she finally stood up for herself. She seemed like the type that took a lot of shit off of people and never spoke up. The look on her face said that she didn't know how this was about to go, but she was ready for it to go south if I took it there.

"Look, I'm not really in the mood to deal with this right now," she said, shaking her head and trying to step around me, but I blocked her path. Even though I should have been out here worried about Troy, it didn't feel right to just let her walk off.

"I'm sorry that bitch just did you dirty in there. That shit was fucked up."

She squinted up at me in suspicion like she was trying to

figure me out, and I took that moment to soak up her beauty again. Just like earlier, she had her hair pulled up on top of her head in a bun that looked like she hadn't put much thought into it, making her beautiful cocoa face more visible. Her stress filled eyes were slanted and dark brown, almost black, giving her an exotic look. She bit into her plump heart shaped lips as I appraised her from the top of her head down to the worn-out walking shoes she wore. And just like before, I was amazed by her natural beauty.

"Yeah, well I find that hard to believe after I fucked up yo' car and ran," she muttered bitterly, once again trying to get by and again, I stepped in her way.

"So, you think it's okay to go around fuckin' shit up and not payin' for it?" I questioned with my head cocked to the side.

I didn't know what to say to make her give me some of her time. Granted, she was pissed off and tryna get up outta here, but it still hadn't ever been this hard to talk to a woman for me. She didn't seem like she would fall for the normal shit I did or said when I was trying to get a bitch number. Hell, she probably thought I only wanted her shit cause of the accident, but it was way more to it than that. I'd only seen this girl twice and both times it was some crazy shit happening, but something about her was pulling me in.

"And if I do?" She sassed, rolling her neck. "You lil niggas go around fuckin' shit up every day and not payin' for or caring who gets hurt."

"Lil niggas? Ain't shit lil bout me, shorty." She rolled her eyes like she'd heard that shit a thousand times, and she probably had. Niggas out here stayed bragging on their dick. The thing was, I wasn't lying. I could probably fuck the atti-tude right out of her, and I definitely planned on trying to.

"Wooow, that's original." She laughed, shaking her head

and trying to walk off, but this time I grabbed her by the arm, stopping her from getting too far away.

"Aye, wait!"

"What do you want from me, huh? I don't have insurance, okay! That's why I lied. You wouldn't even get shit but my raggedy ass car if you sued me, so what do you want?" She looked fed up and tired.

For some reason, I wanted to make things all better for her. I never felt like that for anybody besides my OG and my sister. I wasn't cruel or nothing, but most times I saw somebody struggling, I felt like that was on them. It had to be something they did to get them there, right? I didn't even know this girl's real name, and I was out here tryna keep her from leaving while my boy was upstairs in surgery. See how she had my head all fucked up in one day?

"I don't know," I admitted letting out a deep breath. "I'm just tryna look out, shorty."

"For what? You don't know me, and you don't owe me shit!" She hissed and then bucked her eyes at me like she was just now realizing something. "You tryna fuck? Is that why you tryna look out? Cause you think you gone get some pussy out the deal?"

It took me a second to realize that she was for real, and my mood instantly changed from nice guy to asshole.

"You think I gotta do all this for some pussy?" I asked, shaking my head in disbelief. "My homie upstairs with a bullet in his chest, but I'm out here wit' yo' ungrateful ass tryna make sure you straight. A nigga thought maybe you was different and could use some help but fuck it!" Shrugging, I let her arm go and headed back into the hospital, not even waiting on her to say shit. Maybe she was used to niggas expecting shit in return for the attention they gave her, but she had me fucked up. I didn't need to give a bitch shit to get the pussy. One phone call and I could have two bitches ready to fuck right now with no questions asked. And she thought I needed to offer her something for sex.

Real shit, I felt offended and it took a lot to offend me considering that I was a street nigga turned rapper. I passed back by the nurses' station where the same three women were still standing around going back and forth over shorty that had left. The me that had wanted to help her would have stopped and told them about themselves, but the side of me that was pissed and didn't give a fuck let me whisk right past.

Pree stood up when he saw me coming and met me half-way. "They still ain't came out and said nothin', young blood," he sighed.

"How fuckin' long it take to get a bullet out?" I growled as we made it back to where he'd been sitting. I plopped down in the seat next to him but shot right back up and started pacing. Pree just sat there looking just as calm as he had when we first arrived.

"It takes however long they need to be careful so yo' boy don't die," he answered, getting comfortable like he knew we would be there for a while. I tried to let his words sink in, so that I could calm down, but that shit wasn't working. Me and Troy had gotten into plenty of shit in the past, but both of us had come out fine; never getting shot or hurt for that matter. It was like we had an angel looking out for us all this time. "Sit yo' ass down, nigga. The dicks is here," Pree said only loud enough for me to hear.

Of course, they were called. They always came out for gunshot victims. I wiped the sweat from my face and then sat down, leaving a chair between me and Pree as they approached. They were both wearing some wrinkled ass suits like they slept in them bitches and some cheap ass shoes. The black one was the first to speak, pulling a small notebook out of his pocket. I guess he felt like we would be more receptive to him, but I didn't fuck with the police, and I really didn't fuck with black ones.

"You fellas here with the victim? A Troyvante Smith?" He asked with his pen poised above the paper ready to write.

"Yeah, I brought him in," I let him know, eyeing his partner before giving him my attention again.

"Well, I'm detective Chaney and this is detective Reese. We have a few questions to ask you about the incident."

"He didn't see shit. We were still inside the studio when the shots went off," Pree answered for me, drawing the detectives eyes his way.

"And you are?"

"I'm Pre. I own the studio," he explained in the same even tone. The detectives shared a look before Chaney wrote something else down.

"We'll need to speak with the victim also-"

"He still in surgery. Why don't you leave a card, and I'll have him call when he's up to it?" Pree interrupted, causing them to look at each other again.

"I'm not really-"

"Listen, leave the card and gone 'bout y'all day. Ain't like you really give a fuck what happened to him anyway." Chaney looked like he wanted to object but thought better of it and handed Pree the card before gathering his partner and sulking back out the way they came. As soon as they cleared the double doors, he balled up the tiny card and threw it on the other side of the room. "Bitch ass niggas," he mumbled, leaning his head back against the wall with his eyes closed. I was about to do the same and rest my eyes too, but I saw the doctor who'd been with Troy and met him before he could get all the way in the waiting area.

"Doc, please tell me you got something," I pleaded with the short Indian man. Fixing his glasses on his face, he looked over the chart he held.

"Are you the family of Troyvante Smith?"

"Yeah, that's us," Me and Pree both said at the same time.

"Okay, well the patient had a gunshot wound to the chest. However, the bullet cracked the ribcage and punctured the right lung. We were able to remove it and stabilize Mr. Smith, but he's been put on a ventilator. Mr. Smith has also been put in a medically induced coma to speed along the healing process."

"So, is he gonna be ok?" I asked for clarification. With everything he had just said, all I understood was that my boy was in a coma and he couldn't breathe on his own. The doctor blinked rapidly as he tried to get his words together and pursed his lips into a thin line.

"Right now, it is touch and go. We are hoping that with the help of the ventilator, he will come out of this."

I tuned his ass out after that. He was basically saying that he ain't know if Troy was gon' make it or not. All this because I told them niggas to leave the studio? I felt like this was all my fault. I should have been the one to take that bullet. Their beef was with me, not him. All he had done was back me up, and it was about to cost him his life. I was so pissed off that my hands were shaking, and I had to sit down, so that I could try and get myself under control.

"Ju!" Pree barked, gaining my attention. His face was covered in concern, and I could tell he was searching for the right words, but there were none.

"I swear to God, Pree, I'ma kill them niggas! I swear to fuckin God!" I cried as I wrung my hands. I ain't care who heard me. The way I was feeling right now, I would gladly kill them niggas and go to jail with a smile in every mugshot.

"Ju, I know you upset. Shit, I'm mad as fuck too, but don't be stupid like these other niggas out here. You got a whole future to think about." He threw his hands up defensively when my dark eyes met his. "I ain't saying don't do what needs to be done. I'm just telling you to be smart about that shit. You can't be up in here talking that shit 'cause as soon as something happens to one of them niggas, one of these nosy bitches in here gone be talking 'bout how you were making threats tonight." He lowered his voice and nodded towards the nurses' station where the bitch who had fired shorty stood, pretending to do paperwork. He was right. It would be real fucking stupid to throw my life away by getting caught. I needed to get myself under control and plan this shit out right. I nodded with a heavy sigh, silently letting him know that I was gonna chill.

"The doctor said he can have one visitor right now. You gone head and see him while I call his people's again." He placed a firm hand on my shoulder before walking further down the hall to make his phone calls.

I can't lie, it took me like five minutes to even get up out of the chair. A nigga ain't know if he was prepared for what I might see once I made it to his room. The few little minutes it took me to get to the room he was in felt like forever with the way my feet dragged. I sort of wished that Pree would have come in with me 'cause seeing my nigga on his death bed wasn't something I was sure I could handle. Standing just outside the door of room 205, I closed my eyes and said a quick prayer before pushing my way in.

Despite the wires, IVs and tube in his throat, Troy looked sleep. Like if I dangled a lit blunt in his face, he would wake up grinning and ready to smoke, telling me about some new rhymes he'd come up with. I moved closer to the bed, rubbing my burning eyes and stopped beside him.

"Bro, you gotta pull through this shit, man. Ain't no way I can be out here without my right hand," I told him. "You just worry about gettin' better, and I'ma handle this street shit. On God and everything I love, them nigga's gone feel me." I bumped his limp hand with a pound and exited the room.

It had been awhile since I had done some real street shit, but it was something that never truly left a nigga. For everyday my boy was down, somebody from their camp was getting laid down, innocent or not. That's just how this shit went.

NIVEA

"Ma, ma, ma!" Kymia yelled, coming up on the side of me all dressed in her uniform and the new shoes I'd gotten her. Despite the fact that I had lost my main income the week before, I still went ahead and got them. I had always felt like children shouldn't know of your struggles, so I'd bought the shoes and acted like everything was fine. As far as they were concerned, I'd gotten off early that night last week because they didn't need my help. They even thought I had been on vacation since then and I intended on keeping it that way.

"Yes, Ky?" I asked, trying to hide what I'd been doing on my phone before she could see. My kids were nosy as hell, and they saw everything.

"What you know 'bout Ju Savage, ma?" She asked, laughing with a hand on her hip.

See what I mean? How the hell did she know I was looking at one of his videos? I blacked out the screen on my phone and put it in my back pocket, smacking my lips. "Girl, I was just scrolling through Facebook." I waved her off, but I could still feel her watching me with a knowing grin. The truth was, I had read so much about him and listened to so many of his songs that I knew him well. After he put me in my place last week, I felt bad for assuming the worst, and had spent these last few days thinking about how I would make it up to him if I ever saw him again.

"We met him. Mama hit his car." Quiana came into the kitchen and said, plopping down into her chair at the kitchen table. Shit! I had tried to keep that little bit of information to myself. Kymia's mouth dropped open, and she started doing one of them stupid ass dances.

"We 'bouta be rich! You know how much money he got, ma?!" She asked with wide eyes.

"Ain't nobody 'bouta be rich, Ky. Go sit down so you can eat."

"We woulda been if I was there. I was gone fall straight out the car like, oww, my neck, my back, I can't feel my legs!" She screamed, falling on the floor.

"Girl, get up off that floor before you get them shoes dirty!" I warned with a laugh. She could be so silly sometimes that you would never know she was the same girl who'd just given you attitude. Me saying her shoes would get dirty was all it took for her to get her ass up and into a chair though.

"Y'all sholl know how to kill a nigga's dreams," she grumbled, taking a big bite of the oatmeal I had made for them.

"Mama, when I'm getting some new shoes?" Quiana asked innocently. Of course, she would be expecting some too.

"Next paycheck, baby girl."

She seemed happy with that answer and resumed eating with a nod. I was glad that QJ was much less into keeping up with his sisters or else he would have been next asking for more shoes. Toddlers were much easier to please than preteens and teenagers. Speaking of my little man, it was time to get him up. I left the girls in the kitchen and walked through my small two-bedroom apartment until I got to my room. He was still sleeping with his arms propped behind his head just like his father. It was crazy how much he was like him, even down to the way he used to sleep. Suddenly, a wave of sadness fell over me thinking about their father. Quad was a street nigga through and through. Since I'd met him, he had been in and out of jail, always looking for the next come up. Despite that, when things were good, they were really good. He always somehow managed to take care of things when he was around. He had treated Kymia like she was his from the beginning and was there for everything that her real daddy wasn't. Back then, he was robbing gas stations and making good money by my standards. Even though I was terrified for him, Ky and myself, he assured me that he wouldn't get caught. And he didn't until he decided to outdo himself and rob a currency exchange. Two weeks after getting away with thirty thousand dollars, the police busted into his brother's apartment where he was staying until the heat died down and carted him straight off to jail. That was the first bid I did with him. And I was faithfully writing letters, sending money and dragging Kymia up there for visits twice a week.

When he got out, he swore that he had a better hustle; one that was gonna get us just as much money, but with less of a risk. That turned out to be selling drugs for a local street king by the name of Supreme. These were his words, not mine. I can't lie, he was doing good, and we were living somewhat lavishly. Things were going so good that when I popped up pregnant with Quiana, I wasn't worried at all. Quad moved us into a three-bedroom ranch out in Calumet Park, told me to give him a couple years, and we'd be living out in Olympia Field. I believed him. Why shouldn't I have? Everything he had said so far had turned out to be true.

We were still in the middle of decorating our house and making plans for Quiana's birth when he got caught selling to an undercover police. I was a month away from my due date and didn't know what to expect. Quad told me that everything would be alright and that Supreme would take care of me, but that never happened. He ended up having to serve three years and some change, and I ended up getting put out and having to move my two kids in with my mama.

I stopped waiting on Supreme to come through after that and did what I had to do, which was getting a job. Besides, my mama wasn't gone let me stay there without doing nothing with two kids eating her out of house and home; her words not mine. She had enough of that with Nadia coming and going every couple of months.

It didn't even take me a year to get me and my kids out of there. And even with my meager earnings, I was able to handle taking care of us and still looking out for Quad since Supreme had basically turned his back on him. Once again, I was traveling back and forth up to the prison, but with two kids this time, writing letters and sending pictures too. When Quad was finally released right before Quiana turned four, I was done with easy money. We'd both gotten a little bit older and our responsibilities had changed, so I was adamant about him getting a job and us doing things the right way. Quad agreed and started filling out applications, but nobody wanted to hire a two-time felon.

I tried to encourage him every time he was rejected, but his pride was shot. No real man wanted to have his woman taking care of all the bills, the kids and him. I'll give him credit for trying to live right, but after six months of being denied, Quad went right back to doing what he always did. I guess in hindsight, I couldn't blame him or any other black man that had been imprisoned and couldn't function in regular society, but that didn't mean I wasn't angry about it. Since Supreme wouldn't fuck with him and had encouraged nobody else to either, Quad went right back to robbing stores and shit. He wasn't getting as much as before considering that he wasn't hitting them as often. I guess in his mind he thought that if he spread them out then he would be less likely to get caught. As crazy as it sounded, it did work. They never actually caught him for the robberies, but they did catch him for trying to buy some weight with the money he had stolen not even two years later.

He had to use all of the money he had stashed to get out and get a lawyer. He warned me that he would have to do time for this one though. Like, real time. The lawyer was able to buy him almost a year and a half while he filed paperwork and pushed back court dates but eventually, he ended up with ten years.

QJ was damn near one when he had to turn himself in and I was once again stuck with another baby by myself. I handled it like always. Knowing that I had at least eight more years to go doing this on my own was rough. There was nothing that Quad could promise me at this point; no reassurances that he could make. I was just going to have to ride this out and hope that with age came maturity for him because our kids would be grown by the time he was set free.

Almost as if he knew I was thinking about him, my phone rang with a collect call from Statesville prison. I wiped the tears that had formed in my eyes and tried to get myself together before I pressed one to accept.

"Hey beautiful." His deep baritone filled my ear, causing me to smile.

"Hey, baby daddy." I gushed. Regardless of how down I felt, he could always make me feel better, even with something as simple as a compliment.

"What you doin'? What the kids doin'?" He asked, and I could tell he was grinning. I walked the short distance to where QJ was still laying knocked out and shook him awake gently. It never took much to get his little bad butt up. As soon as he felt me touch him, his eyes popped right open.

"I literally just woke Quad up, but the girls are eating breakfast. Say hey to yo' daddy, QJ." I told him once he was sitting up. Hearing that his daddy was on the phone instantly gained a bunch of giggles out of him.

"Daddy! Hey daddy!" He squealed, trying to take the phone from my hands. I placed it to his ear so that they could talk while I grabbed him some clothes out of the dresser we shared. It was already feeling like it was going to be a scorching hot day, so I pulled out a pair of tan cargo shorts and a white collared shirt. I hurried to get him dressed while he tried to tell his daddy about his day at school yesterday mixed in with a little bit of last week. It didn't take long for me to hear Quad telling him to give me the phone. Qj played around like he didn't hear him, still trying to talk, but I snatched the phone away in enough time to hear Quad laughing at his antics.

"Boy, put yo' mama on the phone and quit playin'."

"I got it bae." I sighed tucking the phone between my head and shoulder as I tied QJ's shoes, then told him to go into the kitchen to eat. He took off running while I put his pajamas into the hamper and followed him out.

"Awe damn, you did say you made breakfast. What you cook?" Quad asked, just making conversation.

"The lies! I ain't say I cooked shit. They eating oatmeal!" I chuckled. I didn't have time every morning to make them a big breakfast. They were lucky if I was able to cook twice a week.

"Damnnnnn, that's what I ate this morning. Nigga, stop feeding my kids like they in prison." He scolded with a laugh.

"Yeah a'ight, as busy as I be! Microwave food is my best friend."

"Yeah, I know, ma. I was just fuckin' with you. I couldn't

even imagine doing all the shit you do and taking care of the kids. You definitely out there doing yo' thing. I just wish I was there to help you out." His voice filled with sadness. I knew that he felt some type of way about not being able to help and missing out on so much of the kids' lives. It seemed like every other time we talked, he went from feeling bad about the situation to making me feel guilty about being free. I guess this was one of his sad days. I hadn't ever been locked up before, but it must take a mental toll on people because Quad's attitudes fluctuated damn near on a daily basis.

"I know, bae. I wish were you was here too," I said, setting a warm bowl of oatmeal in front of QJ. This was becoming routine for me to use kiddy gloves with Quad's feelings when I really wanted to tell him that this was his fault. He was the one who ruined his record repeatedly and couldn't get a job, but shit like that would cause an argument.

"Aye, you around the girls? Tell 'em I love them."

Turning to the girls, I braced myself for their reaction to Quad. Usually, Quiana was excited to hear from her dad. Despite him being in and out of jail, all she had of him were good memories. Now Kymia, on the other hand, wanted nothing to do with him. I didn't know if it was because she was older and had been affected by his broken promises or if it was because she knew of more than just the good. Whatever it was had her not wanting to acknowledge Quad at all.

"Girls, daddy said he loves y'all."

Of course, Kymia rolled her eyes, but said nothing while Quiana excitedly said she loved him too. As usual, I lied. "They said they love you too, bae." I ignored Kymia's hard stare as I collected their dishes from the table.

"Y'all comin' up here this weekend, right?" He asked, sounding hopeful. I hadn't told him about me losing my job yet or the accident. I didn't want him to know how in one day I took two losses, since the repairs for my car was like

$700. There was no way I could afford that with just my cleaning job. We had been riding the bus or pooling with Niyah. Thankfully, today was one of the days that she could drive me to drop the kids off. I didn't have to work today, so I planned on filling out as many apps as I could.

"I'm gonna try, a'ight? I don't know if I will have enough gas after I pay the rent." He sighed deeply, letting me know that he was disappointed, but there was nothing I could do.

"A'ight man. I just really wanna see y'all... I miss-" He started but was interrupted by the automated voice telling us that we had one-minute left. "Damn, I hate this part."

"Yeah, me too." My voice dropped an octave and sadness filled me. It was always hard to hang up, especially when we were having such a good conversation. "I love you."

"I love you too, ma." He managed to get out before the phone clicked off. I didn't even have time to relish the comfort of his voice before I had to get back into Mom mode. Checking the time on my phone, I saw that we had less than fifteen minutes to be out the door.

"Okay y'all, we gotta go. Niyah should be pulling up any minute," I ordered, helping QJ down from his seat and taking him into the small bathroom so that I could wipe his hands and face. I helped him brush his teeth quick and by the time I was done, the girls were standing at the door with their bags.

I gave them all a quick once over, grabbed QJ's book bag off of the hook and slid on my shoes just as Saniyah messaged me to say she was pulling up.

"Hey yall!" She said excitedly as we all filed into her car.

"Hey Niyah!" Quiana and Qj both gushed while Kymia let out a dry ass hey. She was probably still in a mood about me telling Quad she loved him. By the time she got out of school, she would have something else to be upset about.

"Hey boo," I greeted her, opening up the email I'd just gotten. "Oh shit! I passed my final!"

I did a little dance in my seat while Saniyah clapped. After all of the stress this past week, I had still managed to pass, and now I was that much closer to my dream.

"Yasss bitch! You know we gotta go out and celebrate, right? And before you try and come up with an excuse, don't! You definitely going," she said and for the first time, I didn't feel like arguing with her. I did deserve a night out, and I was gonna take one.

SAVAGE

$\mathcal{I}$ sat in VIP barely boppin' my head to the new 6ix9ine that they had blasting. Word was, The Goon Squad and their peoples was supposed to be making an appearance, and I planned on laying more than a few of them down. It had been a week and Troy's condition hadn't changed, which only made me seek revenge even more. Mone was pissed at me 'cause I had missed a recording session and a performance at this shit called "Kick-Off the Summer".

What he didn't understand was that even though I fucked with this rap shit, it wasn't my life. He gave me a long ass speech about not letting the streets pull me in and fuck up this opportunity, but I wasn't trying to hear that shit. I had spent my whole life without a father, and I ain't need him to step in and fill the role. My life was just fine, and it was gone be even better after I handled these niggas for Troy.

I was laid up in the cut in a position that allowed me to see the entire club as I nursed a bottle of Hennessey. It was already going on 1 a.m. and these dumb ass niggas still hadn't showed up. I didn't know what time they were planning on making their entrance, but I was prepared to wait for as long as I needed to. I peeped the bottle girl sashaying my way wearing the fitted black t-shirt and booty shorts that was their uniform. She was looking thick as hell, and the fishnets and bright red heels made her body pop even more.

"Heeeey, Ju daddy!" She purred, stopping in front of me with her hip out. My eyes traveled the length of her, stopping at her face, and I tried not to laugh. Shorty ass was a straight up tip drill. Her face was beat the fuck up and not in a good way. I wondered where this broad had come from 'cause she wasn't the same girl who had been bringing me bottles since I got there.

"Sup." I hit her ugly ass with a head nod and continued to scope out the club, ignoring the look she gave me.

"Wellllll, do you need anything?" She finally asked, bending down so that she was closer to my face. I was even more turned off by the fact that her breath matched her appearance.

"Nah, I'm straight. Beat it, shorty." I held my breath, hoping that she wouldn't put up a fight and be blowing that shit in my face. But, she didn't move; she just smiled and cocked her head to the side.

"No baby. I mean anything." She ran her hand down her chest and raised her eyebrows at me suggestively. My first instinct was to push this hoe out my face, but I didn't need to be getting kicked out of here before them niggas showed up.

"Look shorty, the only thing I need is for you to go brush yo' teeth before you come say shit else to me," I growled. Her head snapped back from the insult, and she scrunched up her face making her look even more hideous.

"First of all, my breath don't stink, and ain't you supposed to be nice to yo' fans?" she quizzed, standing up with her hand on her hip.

"Nah, yo' shit don't just stink! It's foul as fuck! And bottle girls supposed to be fine, but we both see that ain't true!" I spat, glancing at her briefly before returning my gaze to the dancefloor behind her.

"Fuck you, Ju!" She tossed out, spinning on her heels and storming off. That was her best bet before I smacked that crooked wig off her head.

The club was packed, and it was big hoes in here twerking like they were trying to get they rent paid. My nigga Troy would have been up in here turned the fuck up; this shit was definitely his scene. I scanned the slew of women trying to decide which one I would take home if these niggas didn't fall through. I still wasn't fucking with Kisha on that level. And since I'd blocked her number and missed my studio time, she hadn't seen me to try and fuck her way into my good graces. Honestly, I had been so deep into getting at the nigga Jay and who he rolled with that I hadn't even thought about pussy. If I ended up taking one of these bitches to the hotel, she was gone get some 'Fuck up yo' uterus dick'.

I was looking between the door and the dance floor when my eyes landed on a flash of red. Her back was to me, but for some reason, I knew it was shorty from the accident. She was rocking the shit out of the skin tight, red body con dress. The last two times I'd seen her, she had been covered up in work clothes, and even though I could tell that she had a nice body, I wasn't prepared for what I was seeing. Shorty was filling the fuck out of that little ass dress.

I ain't even realize how I leaned forward, so that I could get a closer look when she danced her way around to face me. She was all made up, looking almost golden on some Egyptian shit with her shoulder length hair parted down the middle and flowing every time she tossed her head. While all these other bitches were in here grinding and twerking all on the floor and shit, she was swaying and slow winding to some soft ass Jacquees joint. That had to be the sexiest shit I ever seen in my whole life. I don't know if I was drunk or what, but when she threw her head back with her eyes closed, I couldn't stop myself. It was like my feet were moving on their own. It ain't even matter that the last time I saw her she pissed me off. Or that I still ain't know her real name. Something about her spoke to me.

I kept my eyes on her as I made my way through the crowd, brushing bitches off me left and right. I sped my ass up though when I saw some tall goofy looking nigga yoke her ass up and start barking in her face. "Aye, get yo' 'fuckin hands off her!" I gritted, making my presence known as soon as I was close enough. They both looked in my direction, and I could tell by how wide shorty eyes got that she recognized me right away.

"Mind yo' business. This between me and my baby mama!" He was already back in her face before he even finished the sentence. I pushed my tongue into my cheek and tried to control my anger, but that shit wasn't working. I ain't never liked a nigga turning his back on me. It was always some wanna be tough ass nigga that talked the most shit but wasn't really bout this life. I already knew he was pussy, and that was confirmed when I upped my banger and put it against the back of his head. His body stiffened up quick as hell when he felt that cold steel and he put his hands up instinctively. At the sight of a gun, the crowd around us thinned out, and a chorus of shrieks replaced the music.

"You gone shoot me ova this bitch?" He asked, turning around slowly and nudging his head in her direction.

"Nah, I got more important shit to risk my freedom on, but I am gone beat yo' ass though." I hit him across his shit with the butt of my gun before he could even register what I had said, making him drop to his knees. The flash from people's phones went off as I hit him with a two piece and left him snoring while shorty pulled at my arm.

"Oh my God! Stop, Judah!" She screamed with tears running down her face. I snatched away, all of a sudden pissed. Pissed at myself for forgetting what I was here for and pissed at her for pulling me off that nigga.

"Fuck you tryna help this nigga for?"

"I'm, I'm not. I don't want you to get in trouble!" She yelled, sweeping her arm out towards the crowd of people recording and taking pictures. Shit! Mone was gonna be pissed about having to clean this shit up.

"What the fuck! Nivea, are you okay?" Some caramel skinned shorty pushed her way through and asked with worry all over her face as she took in the scene.

"She's fine!" I answered before Nivea could and pulled her closer to me. "I got her, a'ight." I didn't even wait for her to say shit else, I just turned and walked away with shorty's hand wrapped securely in mine. She didn't even put up a fight as we weaved our way out of the club through niggas trying to dap me up and bitches screaming my name.

We made it all the way to my car and was pulling off before I even addressed her. "Fuck was you doin' in the club after yo' ass just lost yo' job!? Swear yo' ass just keep on provin' me right, Nivea!" I growled, glad to finally be able to put a name to her face.

She'd surprised me when she called me Judah. Nobody but my OG and my little sister called me that. Everybody else knew better. Still though, it sounded good as hell when she said it, even though she was hysterical. She sat up against the passenger side door breathing hard and looking at me like I was crazy. "You got a kid and shit at home while you out here getting hemmed up and shit."

"You don't know shit about me." She smacked her lips.

"Why do you even keep making me yo' business if I'm just like all these other hoes out here!"

"I already told yo' ass, I don't know!" I let out a sigh, realizing that I was probably scaring her. "Listen, just tell me where you live, so I can take you home and make sure you get in safe." Her eyebrows shot up quick as hell, and she started shaking her head at me.

"Hell naw! I don't know you. I damn sure ain't telling you where me and my kids live!"

Kids? Her adding a plural to the word had me inspecting her body again. It damn sure ain't look like she had kids. Her body didn't give it away and neither did her young ass face. Then again, her ass could have been wearing one of them training things, and she could have started young on her shorties. It wouldn't have been shit I hadn't ever seen before. It was girls out here having babies before they even got out the eighth grade. Still, I didn't take her as that type of female. She carried herself in a way that didn't come off like some of these other young ass mothers out here hiding kids and shit.

"You know my government and I know yours," I shrugged. "That's all you need to know. Besides, half the club just seen me leave with you," I stated the obvious. She seemed to be thinking it over as I cruised down 79th street then stopped at a light and looked over, waiting on her reply.

"Make a left up here," she finally told me, relaxing enough to sit back and put on her seat belt. "I live right over on 82nd and Ashland."

She ain't say nothing else while I drove the short distance over to her street, and I didn't either. I kept stealing glances at her as she stared quietly out of the window. Probably trying to figure out how her night had ended with her baby daddy getting his ass beat and her getting a ride home from me. Real shit, I didn't know what the fuck had happened either. Shorty had a way about her that had me out here reckless and just not giving a fuck about nothing but her when she was around. My phone vibrated in my pocket, and I pulled it out to see a ton of missed calls from Mone, Pree, and an unknown number. They must have heard about the shit back at the club and since I didn't feel like dealing with either one of them, I tucked that shit back in my pocket.

"Right here, right here," Nivea said, breaking me out of my thoughts. I pulled my rental over right in front of her building and mugged the ten niggas that stood out front. Seeing the look on my face, she let out a small chuckle like they were harmless or something.

"I'ma walk you up." I let her know and got out before she could protest. Their loud chatter stopped when I stepped around the car and met her on the other side. I gestured for her to lead the way and followed her up the walkway.

"Oh shit! That's Ju!" One called out as we passed them.

"Damn, sup Ju."

"That Gotti remix the shit man!"

They all got geeked seeing me out here. I ignored the awe in their voices and gave Nivea's ass all of my attention until she stopped to unlock the door that led into her building. When I finally looked away, I saw that mine weren't the only eyes on her, instantly gaining an attitude from me.

"Aye! Y'all lil niggas can't be out here no more," I warned, staring them all down. They couldn't have been no older than 16 anyway.

"But, Ju man, I live here tho'."

I turned to see the smallest one out the bunch with his face all frowned up as he pulled up the baggy sweat pants he wore. "Nigga, so take they ass inside yo' crib then. Lil young asses ain't got no business out here no way," I grumbled, barely flexing at his little scary ass.

"A'ight man," he whined and cowarded away. His friends all

sucked their teeth and mumbled about it being bullshit, but I bet when I came back out ,they was gone be gone. I turned back to Nivea as she held the door open for me, shaking her head.

"What?" I hunched my shoulders and stepped inside behind her. By now, I could barely feel the effects of the Hennessey I'd been downing at the club, but I could tell that she was still good and bubbly now that the excitement had died down.

"Them lil boys ain't hurtin' nobody." She giggled over her shoulder as I followed her up the stairs. It seemed like she was putting an extra switch in her hips the way her ass was jiggling. I adjusted my semi hard dick in my Balmain jeans and tried not to think about digging her little ass out.

"Still shouldn't be out there looking all at yo' ass and shit," I mused, more so to myself than her. She let out another one of them girly ass giggles that would have normally bugged me but was cute coming from her. It was extra feminine and flirty, not all forced and shit. She threw her head back in laughter this time like I'd said the funniest shit ever, and damn near fell up the last step.

"Let me find out you jealous of some lil ass kids, Ju Savage." She teased as I helped her to her feet and pulled her body into mine. *Damn, she smells good as hell!* I thought as whatever fruity ass scent she wore filled my nose.

"Fuuuuck," I moaned under my breath, trying hard not to think with my little head. "Which...uhhh, door is yours, ma?" My words were coming out jumbled and shit like I was a straight virgin out here. My dick thumped against my zipper, trying to let it be known that it was time to fuck. A nigga ain't never been this close to some pussy I wanted and didn't get it, but I ain't wanna treat Nivea like anybody else. Truth was, this shit was so new to me, I didn't really know how I wanted to treat her, but I knew I didn't want her to be just another fuck. She wasn't letting me off the hook that easy though.

"2108." Her voice came out breathy as hell, and I could feel her heart beating fast against my chest as she pushed herself closer against me.

Don't do it Ju! Don't do it! I kept chanting that shit over and over in my head as I walked her to the door she'd said to go to. I ignored how soft her body was feeling while she stuck the key in the lock and pushed the door open, causing us both to fall in. I ain't have no intentions on coming inside. It wasn't no way I was gonna leave without putting this dick in her life if I did. But shorty turned on me before the door could even click closed and pushed me up against the wall aggressive as hell. Her lips were on mine, and her hands were roaming my chest. Off instinct, I was kissing her back and pulling at her dress, forgetting how just a second ago I was supposed to be leaving. I stooped down and lifted her up by her legs, wrapping them around my waist as I walked through her short hallway, kicking at doors until I found her room.

Her pussy was so hot I could feel it through the two shirts I wore as she grinded against me, and we landed on her bed, making it squeak loudly. I broke our kiss long enough to pull my shirt over my head before hovering on top of her body and kissing my way from her neck down to her small breasts. Giving each one attention, I dipped a finger into her lacy panties and damn near came from how wet she was. Shorty literally had a puddle in her shit. I glanced up to see her head thrown back in passion while her mouth hung open as she released a moan. My dick was so damn hard, I ain't think I would be able to get it out of my pants. I looked around her room to try and calm down some as I played between her folds.

For her shit to be meager, it was neat and clean. She had a

few pictures on the wall of some African shit to match the deep browns and oranges that seemed to be her theme. I continued to skim the room until my eyes landed on the picture that rested on her nightstand. It wasn't even her and her bitch ass baby daddy (who wasn't the same nigga from the club). It was the three smiling kids that stopped my fingers from continuing their exploration. Shorty ass ain't have just one or two kids; her ass had three. One that looked bout grown as me. Swear to God I snatched my hand back like her ass was contagious. Shit, as far as I was concerned, she was contagious as fertile as she was. My face frowned up as I tried to figure out how old she could be with a kid that damn big. I ignored the look of confusion on her face and her calling out to me as I snatched my shirt up and all but ran outta there. I didn't slow down until I was in front of her building where the crowd of little niggas had disappeared. *At least something went my way tonight.* Was all I could think about as I pulled away with no plans on returning.

NIVEA

I woke up to knocking and assumed that it was Saniyah at the door trying to make sure I was okay. The way Judah had run his ass up outta there, I knew it couldn't be him. That's why I just opened it without looking and turned straight back for my bed. My head was pounding from all the drinks Saniyah had fed me at the club and all I wanted was some more sleep. Besides being hungover, I was embarrassed. I didn't know what exactly I had done to him, but whatever it was must have turned him all the way off. I was a little rusty considering that I hadn't had sex since Quad went to jail. But I was sure it wasn't bad enough that the nigga ran from me.

"Saniyah, I need a minute girl. All that drinking wasn't the move, but when I get up, I gotta tell you about Ju's childish ass," I spat, still walking until I was back in my room.

"What about me, shorty?"

I turned around fast as hell when I heard his voice. His dark eyes looked me over expectantly like he was waiting to see what I had to say. I kid you not, just like that, my headache was gone.

"Why you here? Huh? You don't think you embarrassed me enough earlier?" I asked, angrily pulling my short, worn out robe tighter around my body. I don't even know why I was so mad. I'd been in my early twenties before and niggas around that age weren't mature at all. He probably got turned off by something stupid like my stretch marks, or my small slightly sagging breasts. There was really no telling. "Well?"

He stood there staring at me hard, not saying anything like he had the nerve to be upset. Tired of waiting on an answer that wouldn't come, I went to get back in bed with my robe still on, but he grabbed me by the wrist and spun me around to face him. He gazed into my eyes with the same look of anger before they finally softened.

"I ain't mean to hurt your feelings, ma. That shit was me questioning my own moves," he said, leaning down to kiss me, but I turned my head and his lips landed on my cheek. "How you ain't know a nigga wanted you when my dick gets this hard in yo' presence." He pushed himself into me so that I could feel his hardness on my stomach.

The little bit of fight I had in me faded when he wrapped his arms around me and ran his hot tongue from my jawline to my ear, sucking the lobe into his mouth. He backed me up until I fell backwards on the bed and then untied my robe, leaving me in just my cami and boy shorts. Normally, I would have felt self-conscious showing this much of myself in a room illuminated by light. But the way he was devouring me with his eyes, there was no need. Tossing his shirt aside, he bent down and tugged at my panties with his teeth until they were around my ankles.

"Judah," I whispered, moving to sit up. Now that the alcohol wasn't a factor, I was a little more unsure of giving myself to him so soon, if ever.

"Nah, let me taste you, shorty," he whispered, placing a

kiss on the inside of each of my thighs. I could feel his cool breath as he hovered over my center, causing my clit to ache. Even knowing what he was about to do, I wasn't prepared for his mouth on me. He licked at my yoni gently and then sucked her into his mouth. My back arched off the bed, drawing me closer to him as heat erupted from my toes to my head and my stomach clenched. I moaned as he continued to alternate between lapping and sucking until he stuck a finger inside of me, and I couldn't hold it anymore.

"Judahhhhh!" I called out as my body twitched from the aftershock. My heart was pounding in my ears, and I was struggling to get my breathing under control when he popped up with a cocky smirk.

"Now you 'bouta get this real work," he boasted, standing up totally naked with his dick pointing right at me. It was so fucking pretty, I couldn't wait to taste it. I sat up quickly poised to take him into my mouth-

Whap!!!

A ton of stars clouded my vision as I sat up in bed ready to slap the shit out of Judah but wasn't nobody there but QJ's little bad ass. I mugged him and thought about thumping his damn nose for hitting me in the eye but took a deep breath to calm myself down. It served me right for sitting here dreaming about Judah's old nothing ass. I'd been having dreams for the last few nights of him coming back that night and fucking me into a coma. Truth was, I hadn't spoken to him since that night, and I still couldn't figure out why the fuck he had left me here all hot and shit. I was too embarrassed to tell Saniyah about it, so I just told her that he dropped me off at home and left.

Who wants to tell somebody that they had a fine ass rapper in their crib, and he ran away from them? Letting out a deep breath, I sat up and dismissed my alarm since it was set to go off soon before getting out of bed and heading into the kitchen to make the kids some cereal. I stopped by the girl's room and woke them up on my way.

After their bowls were fixed, I went into the bathroom and took myself a cold shower to hose down the fire Judah had unintentionally set. I needed to just let thoughts of me and him go. He obviously had some issues besides being young as hell, and I had too much going on to help him sort it out. I grabbed my washcloth and slathered it with dove before washing my body three times and getting out. Trying to relax my heart rate and get myself under control didn't take as long under a cold spray.

When I was finished, I wrapped myself up in my pink towel, quickly brushed my teeth, and peeked in on the girls to see them both heading to the kitchen fully dressed. I had an interview today for a bakery I didn't even know I had applied to, but I wasn't going to argue with the lady who called when I needed the money. I hurried back into my room and lotioned myself down with coconut oil and dove lotion before slipping on a pair of black, linen capris and white collared shirt. Tossing a pair of black flats into my bag, I proceeded to comb my wrap down, and add a pair of fake pearl earrings and a matching necklace. I added some clear gloss and my look was complete.

QJ's clothes were already set out so it didn't even take me five minutes to get him up, dressed, and sitting at the table with his sisters.

"You look pretty, ma," Quiana complimented me when she looked up from her bowl of cereal, drawing the attention of Kymia.

"Yeah, you do look pretty. Where you goin'?" Kymia looked at me suspiciously. I thanked them for their compliments and poured me a cup of coffee.

"I'm going to an interview. Y'all keep y'all fingers crossed that I get it," I told them, downing the small cup I held. The fact that I hadn't applied had me nervous that the lady was going to figure out her mistake and put me out of her bakery. I prayed that she didn't though because the pay was too good for me to pass up. My phone vibrated against the counter, and I silenced the call. For some reason, I couldn't talk to Quad because I felt guilty about how close me and Judah had come to having sex. And if that wasn't bad enough, I was constantly dreaming about him. I'd already missed two visits, and I know he was calling to curse my ass out. It was hard for me to lie to Quad though, and it seemed like the longer I went without talking to or visiting him, the harder it was going to be to explain why.

The kids finished their food and went to brush their teeth while I texted Saniyah to see if she was on her way. We finished our morning routine with fifteen minutes to spare and were standing outside waiting on Saniyah to pull up. The fact that the little boy from the apartment underneath me and his friends weren't out loitering wasn't missed by me. Even though I'd told Judah to leave them alone, I was glad they weren't out there eyeballing me and Kymia. Most times that we were out together, niggas were trying to come at me and her like I wasn't her whole mama out this bitch. I guess I could thank Judah for that, but my petty side didn't want to acknowledge him at all.

Saniyah pulled up right then, blowing her horn and smiling all hard like the morning person she was. "Hey y'all! You ready to go to this stolen interview?" She asked, laughing.

"Shut up, heffa!" I chuckled. "God set that up. He knew my ass needed a job, so he was looking out." She looked at me sideways and pulled off away from my building.

"Whatever helps yo' thievin' ass sleep at night girl," she cracked, turning up the radio and jamming to Cardi B's new song. I let it go and sang along with her since I'd learned a few new songs when I looked up Ju on YouTube. I couldn't lie, some of the songs I'd listened to were pretty good, and I had gained a new appreciation for rap. Especially when I saw how fine some of them were. Not better looking than Judah, but still fine.

"Let me find out you got a lil Savage in yo' life and you turned out, bitch?" Saniyah said once we'd dropped all the kids off. Looking at her, I could tell she had been dying to get that off her chest since we'd gotten in the car.

"I don't know what you talkin' 'bout. Ju dropped me off and I ain't heard from him, so ain't been no Savage in my life." I quipped rolling my eyes in irritation.

"Oh, he Ju now? What happened to Judah?" She cheesed. See why I couldn't stand friends? They were always in your business poking around and bringing up shit you ain't wanna talk about.

"He been Ju. I only called him Judah 'cause I knew he was gone stop beating Ky's ass."

"So, you just knew he was gone stop 'cause you called him by his government, huh? Speaking of which, have you heard from Ky since that night?" She raised her brows up with her nosy ass.

"Nope, and I hope I don't! That's what his ass gets anyway, gone try and check me about being in the club." I ain't wanna hear from his ass, but I sure did want to see what his face was looking like after Judah pieced him up.

"I can't wait to see the black eyes he rockin' 'cause I know Ju got his shit closed!" She cackled, reading my mind. "I keep watching the video. That shit went viral, but Ju's manager, Mone, old shady ass got it taken down."

I clutched my chest worried. "He ain't gone get in trouble, is he?" I wanted to know. Even though I was mad at him, I didn't want Judah to get in trouble, especially when he was fighting to defend me.

"What! Hell naw he ain't gone get in no trouble, Bitch! That's Ju. Ky ass know not to play with that lil nigga. He may be on that rap shit, but he still got too much respect out here for niggas to snitch about anything he do," she said, waving me off.

"Now this bakery should be coming up on the left." She cut the radio down as she brought her car to a slow crawl. Sweet Things bakery was right on the corner, painted pink and white with huge windows that held dozens of baked goods. Everything they had set up looked freshly baked, and I knew I was going to gain a whole bunch of weight if I got this job. "You sure you ain't fuckin with Ju like that?" Saniyah asked, looking at me strangely.

"Bitch no! I told yo' ass he dropped me off and left. Nigga ain't even get out," I lied, slipping my feet into the flats I'd brought with me.

"That musta been one hell of a ride bitch... This is Ju's mama's bakery."

SAVAGE

$\mathcal{I}$ sat beside my homie's hospital bed sipping on a fresh pint of white remy at ten in the morning, waiting on my OG to call and tell me that Nivea had the job. I already knew she was gonna like shorty, but she said she had to meet her first. Even though I wasn't feeling her having half a basketball team of kids and one that was damn near grown, I still wanted to help her out. Seeing my mama struggle to take care of us on her own gave me a respect for single mothers that were actually about their business.

I'd peeped more than just the decorations and family pictures in shorty's crib. Her shit was clean, and I knew it wasn't just 'cause she was expecting somebody to come home with her. I saw her college course books stacked on her dresser, so I knew she was in school. Nivea was working two jobs with three kids and trying to better herself. I couldn't do shit but admire her. Even knowing all that, and feeling the way I felt for her, I wasn't ready to sit down and raise kids. Plus, I still didn't even know how old she was or how involved she was in her other baby daddy Quad's business. Everybody who was anybody in the hood knew that nigga

Quad was a snitch. My gut told me that she didn't know. Hell, she ain't even know who I was, but how did she think his ass was getting such low jail time for shit that should have sat him down for double digits.

On top of all that, I still hadn't been able to find Jay, and I was still avoiding both Mone and Pree's calls. I threw a pill in my mouth and chased it down with a mouthful of remy, then tried to get comfortable in the hard ass chair they had in here. My phone vibrated in my hand and I answered without looking, expecting my OG's voice to come through. However, irritation filled me when Kisha's irky ass started yelling in my ear.

"So, you can't answer the phone, Ju? I haven't seen or talked to you since Troy got shot, and the first time I do see you, yo' ass all over the internet snatching some old bitch out the club!" I pinched the bridge of my nose and slipped down deeper into my seat.

"You blocked, so no I can't answer, and what the fuck you mean some old bitch?" I asked, knowing that Kisha would be too happy to share whatever it was that she knew.

"Exactly what I said, that bitch old! Her ass damn near thirty and she know she ain't got no business being in nobody's club. Her ass needs to be at home takin care of them lil bastards!" She spat angrily. I could hear her moving around where ever she was, probably home or at the studio. Her ass ain't go nowhere else. Damn, Nivea was almost ten years older than me! No wonder I got a different vibe from her than any other female. It was 'cause she was in a different age demographic.

"Watch yo' fuckin' mouth, Kish! Her kids ain't got shit to do with this!" Even though I wasn't happy about some shit with her, I wasn't about to let Kisha's bitter ass talk shit about her or her kids.

"Oh, you takin' up for her and shit? That cougar pussy

must be something else! Tell me something, Ju. How the fuck two weeks ago yo' ass wasn't trying to settle down with me, but now you got a bitch that's about to go through menopause *and* some fuckin' kids!" Her ass was getting loud as hell in my ear. I pulled the phone away 'cause I could hear her ass without even putting her on speaker.

"Kisha, we ain't together and we ain't never been together, so I ain't gotta explain shit to you. I warned you already to stop talkin' ill about shorty. I ain't gone tell you again." I glanced up at Troy to make sure this shit wasn't disturbing him. It seemed like every time I was around him or trying to take care of business on his behalf, some female was coming with drama. My boy was probably laughing at my ass right about now.

"Ohhhhh, Ok! So, you threatening me over this bitch now? That's what we doin', Ju?" She ranted.

Now see, I had already just told this bitch about disrespecting Nivea. It was like she didn't hear me or didn't care. Kisha knew me well enough to know that I put actions behind my words. Maybe that's what she wanted anyway, for me to chase her stupid ass down. Her ass acted just like a kid on some old any attention is better than no attention type shit. I was about to hang up on her ass 'cause she had taken up a full two minutes of my time with goofy shit, but my OG clicked in. I switched lines so quick, I almost dropped my damn phone.

"So, did you like her or what, ma?" I asked, trying to sound all casual about the shit, even though I was eager as fuck.

"Well, hey to you too, Judah," she said dryly, and I could tell she was rolling her eyes.

"My bad, ma. How you doin'?"

"I'm a'ight. How you doing, baby?" Her voice turned happy like she didn't just have an attitude at me a second ago.

"I'm good too, but I'm a grown ass man, ma. Stop calling me a baby," I teased, already knowing what she was about to say.

"Yo' ass ain't too grown to get slapped, Judah. Don't play with me!" I mocked her as she said it. She been telling me that ever since I was eighteen. "Then again, you out here fuckin' women that's damn near thirty with kids. Maybe you are grown!" She cracked, laughing. I swear my mama thought she was cool or some shit. I had to constantly tell her to act her age.

"Man, be cool, Jackie. Ain't nobody fuckin' that girl. I'm just tryna help her out a lil."

"Watch that Jackie shit, lil boy," she said, smacking her lips. "Since when do you wanna help somebody besides me and yo' sister?"

"Quit playing, ma. You know you raised a gentleman. Now did you like her?" I urged impatiently.

"Alright, alright! Yes, I liked the girl! You already knew I was going to. Hell, she reminds me a lil of myself not too long ago." I couldn't help the smile that took over my face knowing that Nivea got the job and was going to be getting paid good enough that she wouldn't have to work two jobs. My OG had it set up where she could pick her hours and even bring the kids if she needed to. I still had another surprise for her, but I was gone give that to her later. Besides, I felt like I owed her an apology from the other night. "So, you really like her, huh?" she questioned, interrupting my thoughts.

I sighed thinking about whether or not I wanted to tell her about the mixed feelings I was having toward Nivea. Since Troy was out of it, I really ain't have nobody to talk to and get advice from about whether or not I should still pursue her. I already knew my OG was gone be on some old woman empowerment shit and try to come at me on Nivea's behalf. But shit, she had always kept shit real with me, and I valued her opinion. "Mannnn, ma, I don't know. Nivea cool and all, but I ain't ready for a ready-made family."

"Ohhh, so you do like her, but you trippin' 'bout her havin' kids." She tsked, and I knew a long ass lecture was coming. "You think she was ready to raise kids on her own? Like girls dream of getting pregnant and then being stuck to take care of them alone cause niggas scared to step up. Swear I wish I could reach through this phone and slap the shit outta you!"

"Nah, that ain't it. I don't think I'm ready. How I'm supposed to know what to do with some kids? I'm too young for that shit."

"Make up your mind, Judah. You can't choose to only be a grown up when it benefits you. The fact that you went out of your way to look out for her tells me that you care. And you caring about her is caring about her kids. Now you think on that before you disrupt that girl's life too much and then try to skip yo' ass on out!" She demanded and then the line went silent, indicating that she'd hung up. I shook my head at how predictable she was. Even though she came straight at me like a true single mother, I could fully understand what she was saying. I did care or at least like Nivea enough to stick my neck out for her. So, that had to mean something, right?

"Yeah, ma," I answered my phone on the first ring when I saw her calling back. I should have known she had something else to say.

"I forgot to tell you to give Troy my love. I'll make sure to go up there tomorrow and clean his room up a bit since them trifling ass CNAs don't never do it." I just laughed at her fussing 'cause she ain't never trusted the CNAs at any hospital.

"Aye a'ight, I'ma call you back," I mumbled, hurrying her off the phone when Pree stuck his head in the door.

Troy ass ain't have nobody. Mone, Pree and my family were his family. He was an only child and his parents were killed in a robbery when he was like twelve. He was placed in like eight foster homes before he turned eighteen, but thankfully, they never moved him too far away from me and my OG. She always did what she could for him because she felt bad about DCFS never giving her custody.

We had come up together though, getting into shit like gangs and tryna sell drugs. When Pree met us, we were just barely eighteen standing out on the block freestyling and shit. He told us he had a studio and if we ever wanted to not just play around with music, we could come through and record something. It had been Troy's idea to take him up on his offer 'cause I wasn't trying to rap for a living. But three years later, I owed how far I'd come to him making me take that chance.

Pree stepped fully into the room and looked down at Troy with a blank face. "No change I see?" He asked, never taking his eyes off of him. I just knew that he was gone come in here snapping about the moves I'd been making, but he seemed preoccupied with heavier thoughts.

"Nah, they did say that they were getting some brain activity, but his eyes ain't open, so that don't really mean shit to me."

He nodded like he understood, and the room fell silent as we both stared at Troy's motionless body. The door being swung open drew our eyes to where a nurse was coming in with her arms full of soap and shit.

"Oh, I'm sorry. I can come back later," she stuttered when she saw us.

"No, you can go ahead. We got some stuff to take care of," Pree told her, motioning for me to follow him out of the room. I ain't know what the fuck he was talking about, but if he was trying to bring up some music shit, I was gonna spazz. Tucking the half empty bottle of Remy into my pocket, I followed him out into the hallway and stood just outside of the door.

"I said we got some shit to handle. It ain't gone get done if you standing here guarding his room," Pree paused his slow stride to tell me before continuing on down the hall. I really wanted to fight him on leaving this building, but I held a lot of respect for Pree. So much so that I pushed myself off of the wall and followed him outside to his car. He was leaned up against it, waiting on me like he knew I was coming.

As soon as I was close enough, he stood up straight and leaned closer to me like we weren't the only people out here. "Have you gotten any closer to finding that nigga Jay?" He asked.

"If I had, then you would have seen that shit on the news, Pree. I thought you brought me out here to take care of some shit?" I frowned, getting irritated by the fact that I hadn't found that nigga all over again.

"We bout to," was all he said before leading me to the back of his car and looking around. He popped the trunk and pointed inside where the nigga I'd seen with Jay at the studio lay tied up with a towel stuffed in his mouth. As soon as the sun's light fell on him, his eyes popped open and he tried to scream. Pree reached inside and hit his ass so hard, I heard his teeth crack before he slammed the trunk back closed. My mouth fell open and I looked at him with wide eyes. This was the most aggressive I'd ever seen Pree act, anything but calm and cool, so I was shocked as fuck.

"Let's go take care of this shit," he said, walking away.

NIVEA

"*W*hoooo! I thought baking was easy." I admonished as I sank down into Saniyah's car. This was my first day at the bakery and Jackie's ass had worked me like a slave. I had no idea that so many people came through a damn bakery in the span of eight hours.

"Yeah, it's clearly not. Girl, you look like you got into a fight with some flour and lost!" joked Saniyah.

I pulled the visor down and saw that I had some flour on my cheek, forehead, and in my hair, which should have been impossible since I had to wear a hair net. I made an attempt to rub it off, but that only made it worse since my arms were covered in it too.

"Nah, just stop before you get that shit all over my car!" She said, still laughing. I started to put some on her, but she was looking cute today in a yellow sundress with gold sandals.

"Shut up. Ain't nobody 'bouta get this shit on yo' car, but I should put some on you though," I teased, acting like I was about to touch her.

"Nah uh, stop playin'!" She shrieked and leaned away

from me. "I'm lookin' too good to be playin' with you today, Nivea!"

"Okay, okay. I quit. Why you lookin' so cute anyway? You got a date?" I pried with a wide smile. Since I met Judah, Saniyah's stories made me think of him doing some of those romantic things for me. I still hadn't seen him since that night at my house, and I was definitely feeling some type of way about that. That's why I was so surprised when we pulled up at the bakery and Saniyah told me it was his mama's.

The way that whole interview was set up, I knew that he had something to do with it, but I was stuck between wanting to thank him and curse him out. I still didn't know how I'd react once I saw his light bright ass.

"Hell naw, I ain't got no date! I was just 'bouta ride down King Dr. And see if I could find me a rapper and run into his shit!" She said with a laugh, but I knew her ass was dead ass serious.

"Stop it!"

"I'm serious! You got Ju wrapped around yo' damn finger and all it took was you fuckin' up his car. If it's that easy, I'll drive straight into the back of the first Camaro I see! And you know his studio over there, so it's rap niggas in and out that bitch!"

"Judah is not wrapped around my nothing," I denied and waved her off. I sure did want him to be though. Between how hot he had me that night at my apartment and them damn dreams I been having, I'd probably cum as soon as he touched me.

"Listen at you, *Judah not wrapped around my nothin'*," she mocked. "Bitch, that nigga got you a whole job and beat Ky's ass for you. Ain't no niggas my age even doing that."

I didn't really know if I believed that or not. Judah had gone out of his way to get me a job with more pay and benefits, and he beat Ky's ass. But, if he was feeling me like that, why did he damn near run up out of my bed? He hadn't even come back or tried to call me. Maybe he just felt sorry for me. I'd hate to think that the only interest Judah had in me was pity. That would make me feel even worse about all the things he'd done.

"I guess, Niyah," I sighed, not really wanting to talk about what Judah's actions meant.

Out of all the things I had to worry about on a daily basis, the thoughts and feelings of a nigga that was years younger than me should have been the least of them. We weren't even in the same phase of life. I was ready to settle down, buy a house, and start a business. Right now, Judah was living the life of a young rapper and probably had no intentions on doing any of those same things. And then there was Quad. He'd been nothing but good to me despite constantly going to jail. Everybody else had turned their backs on him, and I didn't want to be another disappointment when he didn't have anybody else.

Honestly, I loved Quad to death, but with him being gone, I was missing out on a lot of things. I didn't know if I would be able to go another seven years without companionship. Up until Judah came around, I thought I could handle these years like a champ and be waiting for Quad on the other side of those prison doors. Now, I wasn't so sure.

"Nivea! Nivea!"

"Huh?" I blinked rapidly and looked over to see Niyah side eyeing me. "What?"

"Bitch, you ain't heard a damn thing I said." She pursed her lips in irritation. "We been out here in front of yo' mama crib for five minutes."

I whipped my head around to see that we had made it to my mama's house and were just sitting out front. I frowned at the sight of my little sister's car parked right behind hers in the driveway. The last thing I wanted to do on this beautiful day was be bothered by her annoying ass.

"Damn. My mind was on some other shit," I mumbled quietly, trying to buy some time before I had to step foot inside.

"Yeah, it's on that young d you need to be sittin' on." I frowned at Saniyah's mannish ass, and she bucked her eyes right back. "Bitch, what? You know you want to!"

I waved her off, suddenly feeling like dealing with my mama and sister might not be so bad. "Let me hurry up and get these kids." I pushed open the car door and stepped out hurriedly, trying to dust off some of the flour at the same time.

"Whateva, Nivea. Stop running from the truth!" Niyah yelled at my back as I made my way up the stairs and inside my mom's small, two-bedroom house. As soon as I walked in, the smell of greens, cornbread, ribs, sweet potatoes and macaroni smacked me in the face, and my mouth started watering.

"Ma!" I called out, making my way to the kitchen where Nadia was sitting at the table with her face in her phone. She hopped right up when I entered and ran over to me.

"When was you gone tell me you was fuckin' with Ju Savage!" She shrieked, standing between me and the stove.

"I'm not fuckin' with no Ju Savage!" I rolled my eyes with a groan. "Where is mama and the kids?" I tried to change the subject and step around her, but she wasn't having it.

"The kids in the back and ma upstairs sleeping. Now for real, when did you meet him? How y'all start talking? Is it serious?" She bombarded me with questions.

"I just said-"

"Whateva, Niv." She quipped, waving me off. "I seen the video, and it damn sure look like y'all fuckin' around."

"What video?"

"This one." She was all too happy to shove her phone into my hands.

My mouth fell open in shock as I watched Judah beat the shit out of Ky and then drag me out of the club. I had forgotten all about how people were recording us that night. There was no telling how many people had seen this shit. What if somebody that Quad knew had seen it and told him? We hadn't talked in a week. What if he knew and didn't call me because he was mad? My mind was racing, and I needed to sit down because I was feeling faint. I slid into the chair closest to me and let out a low groan.

"What the fuck?"

"No, the question is how the fuck? Ain't you like damn near married to Quad's jailbird ass? Fuck is Ju doin' wit' yo' old prison wife ass?" She cackled, snatching her phone back and taking the seat across from me.

"What the fuck you mean by that?" I sneered with narrowed eyes. She frowned and gave me a duh look like I was stupid or something.

"What you think I mean? Yo' ass got three kids already and you 'bouta be thirty." She tsked. "Ju can have any bitch he wants. Hell, he can definitely have me. Fuck he see in yo' ass?"

I shouldn't have been surprised that this was coming from my rude ass little sister, but I was. If she was thinking like this, imagine what all the people who saw that video and knew me were thinking. I didn't even want to think about any of the comments that were under the actual post. Judah wasn't main stream, but he had enough of a following in Chicago alone that half the city had seen it and probably added their two cents.

"Really, Nadia?"

"Shit, I'm just keepin' it a bill with you. Yo' ass shoulda

seen some of the shit other people was sayin', especially Ky's mad ass." She shrugged.

Ky had seen the video? Suddenly, I had lost my appetite. I ran to the back door and called the kids, ignoring Nadia talking shit behind me. They all looked up when they heard my voice and raced to where I stood holding open the screen for them. Well, all except for Kymia.

"Hey mama!"

"Hey ma!"

Quad and Quiana yelled, giving me hugs as they came in the door while Kymia lagged behind. I gave them both a quick pat on the back and ushered them inside. Despite being irritated about the situation with Judah, I was pleased that both of them still looked clean. I'd dressed them both in plaid, baby blue and white shorts with white t-shirts. It seemed like they always stayed clean for my mama, but if I had them, they would have been dirty five seconds after they got dressed. I ushered them inside, ready to get the fuck out of there before I had to slap Nadia.

"Dang, ma. We gotta leave? We ain't even ate yet," Kymia complained, finally making it through the door.

"Yeah, we need to leave now. I can grab y'all something from McDonald's." That gained cheers from the two little ones, but Kymia still stood by the door with a long face.

"Girl, mama made all that food, so they could eat. She gone be mad as hell if they don't, and I'ma tell her you made them leave hungry because you was in yo' feelings over that video," Nadia said without looking up from her phone. I swear I wanted to slap the shit out of her, but I paused long enough to grab them all some of the food she'd made.

Fifteen minutes later, we were walking out the door and back inside of Saniyah's car. As soon as she saw the look on my face, she frowned. "What's wrong, boo?" She questioned, pulling away from the curb.

"Nadia had that damn video from the club and was talkin' shit about me and you know who," I told her hoping that the kids hadn't caught on to what I was saying.

"Well duh, girl. I told you that shit went viral. So what, though? Messing with you know who is gone have a bunch of cameras in yo' face. You better get used to it." She flipped her 30-inch Brazilian weave over her shoulder and smirked at me.

"We not together, so I shouldn't have to worry about shit like this. And what about Quad?" I looked in the rearview mirror at the kids and they all seemed to be in their own little world while we talked, not paying us any attention.

"What about him? He can't seriously expect you to put yo' life on hold for 10 years while he locked up." Her brows knitted together. I knew she wouldn't understand how I felt about Quad and my decision to stick by him. To the world, it might have seemed like I was a fool, but I truly felt that he was my soulmate. Well, I used to before Judah's ass came around making me question myself.

The fact that I hadn't talked to either of them had me even more confused and all I wanted to do right now was take a nice long bath and sleep. Niyah realized that I didn't want to talk and left me alone for the rest of the short drive to my house from my mama's.

When we pulled up, the kids all jumped out the car and Kymia let them in with her key while I struggled with the bag I had the plates in. I was about to step out when Niyah grabbed ahold of my arm stopping me. "Wait girl." She sighed deeply as I sat back into the seat.

"Yeah?" I still had a slight attitude and didn't want to hear shit about how Quad was no good for me.

"I'm sorry," she started. "I'm not tryna make you feel bad about staying with yo' baby daddy, I swear. All I'm tryna get you to see is you deserve to be happy, even if it's with Ju's young ass. You don't owe Quad yo' life, baby. By the time he gets out, these kids gone be grown and you'll have done it all by yourself because you're scared to move on. Just...please, think about it, ok?" I nodded because I didn't know what to say. She still didn't know about what had happened between me and Judah, so she didn't really understand my reservations about him. I gave her a weak smile and got out, making sure to wave as she pulled off. She had given me a lot of things to think about and I planned on doing just that.

Hours later, all of the kids were in bed and I was on my way right behind them. I'd just gotten out of the tub and was applying my cocoa butter Vaseline lotion when my phone buzzed beside me. I almost dropped the bottle when I saw that it was Quad calling. It was ten at night, so it was definitely a surprise to see the jail's 800 number on my phone's screen. I started to let the call go to voicemail and act like I'd been sleeping if he asked but decided against it. It would be better to just get this conversation out of the way. I'd decided that Saniyah had been right, and maybe it was selfish of Quad to want me to wait on him. I couldn't say if Judah would be the one I moved on with, but I sure wished he was.

"He-hello," I stammered after pressing one to accept the call.

"Hey baby." Quad sighed. "How you doin'?" I noted that he didn't sound upset, just sad as hell. It had me wondering what was going on.

"I'm good, how are you? Why they let you get the phone this late? Is everything okay?" I waited on his response with my heart pounding in my ears.

"I'm fine, Nivea." He breathed, and I could hear the smile in his voice, instantly calming me right down. "I'm cool with the supervisor on third. She be lookin' out sometimes."

Jealousy had my eyes narrowed at that, and I wondered what he was doing for her to "look out" for him like that. He must have already known how my thinking was because his smooth laugh filled my ear. "Don't even trip, Niv. She just cool, a'ight. Besides, shorty very married."

"You say that like if she wasn't, you would fuck her. I hope you remember that you got a whole woman out here waitin' on you!" I spat in irritation. It didn't matter to me that just a second ago I was ready to let this relationship go. The thought of another woman getting what I considered mine had me vexed all of a sudden. Any nigga in jail would probably be willing to give his right arm for some pussy, and as far as I knew, Quad hadn't had any in years. A damn C.O. giving him late night calls had me wondering if he was getting it from her.

"Bae, we ain't never had no issues wit' me steppin' out. Why would I wait until I got behind bars to start?" He soothed. "I'm glad you still rockin' with a nigga like that though. I was up in here worried for a minute."

"Always." I let slip out before I could stop myself. This conversation had just gone completely left, and it was too late to take it back, but I didn't think I wanted to. "You don't have to ever worry about me. I'm always gone be here."

"That's what I like to hear, ma. I swear you don't know how much that means to me."

And just like that, I was right back to square one. We spent the next twenty minutes talking about the future and what our plans were for when he got out. Without intending to, I'd let Quad ring me right back in.

QUAD

"*A*re you finished now?" Desiree asked as soon as I hung up the phone. I ignored the look of irritation on her face and wrapped my arms around her.

"Yeah, I'm done, but you don't need to be doing all that extra ass huffin' and puffin' shit while I'm on the phone with her," I said, giving her a stern look.

"Well, I just don't understand the point of even talking to her anymore when you got me." She frowned. "I'm the one in here making moves for you. I'm the one risking my job and freedom."

"Look, it ain't as easy as you makin' it sound. She got my shorties. Fuck I look like having her take any of the risks you take when my kids depend on her." I knew me saying that would piss her off, but I wasn't about to lie. She could take it however she wanted, but she chose to live her life in the shadows.

I'd met Desiree a few years ago when I was going back and forth to court for this last case. She had been transporting inmates to court from the county 'cause that's where she worked back then. I slipped her my number when the other officer wasn't looking and laid this long dick on her that first night. Back then I already knew that I couldn't inform my way out of the years I was about to face, so I recruited her fast as hell. She was an easy target being that she was a damn near fifty-year old widower with no kids. After I fucked her into submission, it didn't take much to convince her to apply at the prison I knew I was going to.

Shit had been smooth sailing ever since I stepped in this bitch. I had her bringing me drugs, food and money. Pretty much whatever I needed, she took care of, including pussy. I really didn't need Nivea for anything, but the truth was, I loved her. Despite all the things I'd done and had kept secret from her, including the extra money I was getting, I really did love her and my kids. Desiree was just a way to get things that I needed for now. Things I would never ask Nivea to do because I loved and respected her. I didn't have to tell Desiree that though.

"Why don't you just be with that bitch then?" She smacked, rolling her eyes and leaning away from me.

I gritted my teeth together, so that I wouldn't choke this dumb ass bitch. She knew Nivea was off limits, and it wasn't like she didn't know I had a family when we started fucking around. Lately though, she had been bringing up everything she did that Nivea wouldn't or couldn't like she thought that shit would make me up her position. As bad as I wanted to punch her in the face right now, I had a role to play. I took a deep breath and planted a soft kiss on her neck, causing her to let out a moan. I'd been fucking with Desiree long enough to know her spots and her neck was the best one. The sound of her soft whimpers had my dick bricking up through the dark blue prison issued sweats I wore. I couldn't lie. She damn sure had some good pussy and she wasn't bad looking neither. She was tall, at least 5'7' with caramel skin, and long thick hair that I loved pulling on when I fucked her from the back. On top of all that, she was a straight up freak and let me fuck her in any hole I wanted. Just thinking about all the nasty shit she let me do had me more than ready to take her ass down right here at the phones.

"Why you actin' like that, bae? You know you the one I want." I continued to place kisses from her neck down to her shoulder while I squeezed her fat ass.

"Well, act like it then," she murmured, finally giving up the fake ass fighting she was doing. I attacked her mouth and pulled her closer to my still growing erection. "Let me take care of you. Let me show you why I'm the one you need." She pushed me back against the wall and worked my sweats down past my hips, making my dick spring right up. I sucked in a deep breath and held it as she swallowed me whole. Her mouth felt just like a pussy but twenty times better. With my dick stuffed down her throat, she licked my balls and hummed at the same time.

"Suck that shit," I hissed and grabbed the back of her head, making her gag and my dick get even harder. The sound of her slurping and her head skills had me spilling my seeds down her throat in under five minutes.

"Mmmmm," she moaned, wiping her mouth and then licking all of my remaining nut from her fingers like it was cake frosting. That shit was so damn sexy, I almost came again.

"Bend over and grab them ankles," I ordered, pulling her up off her knees and turning her towards the wall. She happily obliged, hurrying to get the pants of her uniform down. My mouth damn near watered at the sight of her round ass tooted in the air, and I had to taste her. I ran my tongue from the front of her pussy to the back before sucking her clit into my mouth.

"Ooooh shit, Quad!" She yelled out in pleasure, and I smacked her on the ass hard enough to leave a print.

"Shut yo' ass up!" I gritted, continuing my assault on her clit until I felt her cream fill my mouth. I licked her dry and then stood up, slamming my dick straight inside her warm walls. Real shit, I couldn't even move right away, her shit was feeling so good.

"Fuck me, bae!" She squeaked, trying to throw herself back. I grabbed her around the waist to make her be still.

"Stop moving," I grunted, attempting to control myself. When she finally realized that I wasn't about to death stroke her until she did what I said, she stopped wiggling and I calmed down enough to start slowly sliding my dick in and out of her.

"Quad, yesssss…" she managed to get out as I picked up speed.

I watched the ripples I was creating across her ass and bit into my bottom lip. Spreading her cheeks, I spit right on her glistening asshole and stuck my thumb deep inside. Her knees buckled, and I felt her muscles contracting as my dick became covered in her juices. I was right behind her after seeing how hard she came. Just before my nut erupted, she turned around, dropped down to her knees and sucked every drop right out of me. A nigga was real life stuck for a minute, so she stuffed me back inside of the state issued boxers I wore and pulled my pants back up.

"Damn, that was so fuckin' good, daddy," she gushed, smiling.

"Right and you the only one I'm tryna give this good dick to, so be smooth and just keep playin' yo' position. A'ight?" I said as she straightened herself up. Once her uniform was back on properly, she put her arms around my neck and pecked my lips.

"I got you, baby," she promised, staring into my eyes. I

could tell she real life had feelings for me, but none of that mattered to me. I was gone use her up until I could get out this bitch and be with Nivea, and maybe even after that. With that thought in mind, I followed her back to my cell, so I could get some sleep. That nut had my ass tired as hell.

SAVAGE

*J*still wasn't any closer to finding Jay, and I was beyond vexed. I'd been knocking off niggas that he ran with on damn near a daily basis with no luck. Not even the nigga that Pree had in the trunk told us shit. He was loyal as hell, I'll give him that. He never cracked, not even when Pree was giving him bone crushing blows that had him crying out in pain and spitting up teeth. I wasn't with all that torture and shit like Pree seemed to be. I had always been the type to hit a nigga across his shit with my pistol a couple times and blow his shit back if he didn't tell me what I wanted to know. But that was just me.

All the shit I'd heard about Pree must have been true because he took dude to a secluded ass factory like his ass was in the mob or some shit. Then made me sit with him while he beat the shit out the nigga for hours and questioned him. Real shit, I was waiting on his ass to pull out some pliers and start torturing him. When Pree had finished, even I cringed at how bad he was beaten. The nigga's face straight looked like some raw ground beef. I had to go ahead and put him out of his misery 'cause that shit looked nasty as hell. I

94

ain't even try to ask Pree about any of that shit, even though I wanted to. I knew him well enough to know that he wasn't gone say nothing until he was ready.

We had been murkin' niggas left and right, tryna figure out what hole Jay's ass was hiding in, and he still hadn't said shit. I wasn't tripping though; it was more help for me. He had even got Mone to agree to leave me alone for the time being and work on this possible contract with GMP (Get Money Productions). I couldn't even be happy about their first offer because my nigga was still out, and I couldn't find the pussy who put him there. Which led me to my current drunk state.

It seemed like the longer it took to find Jay, the more I drank, and the more I drank, the dumber my decisions. Like right now, I was at Kisha's crib. I know I'd said I was done fucking with her after her dumb ass broke my phone and was talking crazy about Nivea, but at the moment, she seemed like a safer bet. I knew I didn't feel shit for her, so there was nothing to lose if shit went left. Nivea, on the other hand, was a headache that I couldn't afford to have right now. I had got her number from my OG and tried to call her after that shit that happened at her house, and she ignored every time. Granted, it was some days after, but it still surprised me that she didn't want to talk. The rejection had me in a bad mood the whole next day, snapping on every-body and being mean as hell, way more than usual. If I was being honest, I was still mad, and that's another reason why I was here with Kisha. In my mind, this was payback for Nivea ignoring me.

"What's wrong, Ju?" Kisha asked, looking up at me from her spot between my legs.

I started to ask her what she was talking about, but my limp dick in her hand let me know. Frustration was written all over her face because none of her regular tricks were working. I wished I could say that it was because of how stressed I was about Jay, but I knew it was because Nivea was on my mind.

"Might be too drunk," I lied with a shrug and took another sip of the Remy I was still holding onto. The way her face frowned up let me know that she ain't believe me. She smacked her lips and leaned back with her arms folded.

"Being drunk ain't never stopped you before," she said with much attitude. "What's really wrong? It's that bitch, ain't it?" She fumed, using my legs to stand up. I looked up at her lazily and my dick ain't even flinch at the lacy, pink corset top and matching panties she wore. She had went all out trying to entice me, but my mind was elsewhere.

"I told you to watch how you come at shorty." I sighed, laying my head back on the couch and closing my eyes. I wasn't in the mood for the shit she was on. Coming over there was supposed to be a distraction, but she was putting my focus on Nivea even more.

"Are you serious right now? I'm standing here in some fuckin' lingerie and you still takin' up for her!" Her voice got louder, and I could feel her staring at me.

That shit right there was my cue to leave. I sat up as quickly as I could with the room spinning and pulled my pants up around my waist. If Kisha's ass wanted to argue, she was gone do that shit by herself. Seeing me start to get dressed changed her tune, but it was too late for all that now.

"Okay, I'm sorry, Ju. I won't say nothin' else about her," she pleaded, pulling at my hoodie.

"Kish, get yo' fuckin hands off me," I said evenly.

It didn't matter what she said, my dick wouldn't even get hard for her, so it wasn't no point in staying. Even though Nivea had been on my mind, Kisha bringing her up only made me want to see her. She was cool and laid back, everything that Kisha wasn't, and that made me feel like maybe I should stop trying to run from her. It was crazy how this whole scene right here made me want Nivea in the worst way.

Kisha's hands dropped off my arm immediately and she took a step back, probably thinking about the last time I told her that. "Well, where are you going? You don't have to leave. Just let me try again."

"Maybe next time, shorty," I lied, ignoring the disappointed look on her face and walking straight out the door. It was one in the morning, and I knew Nivea was sleep, but I was still about to go over there. She wasn't too far from where Kisha stayed so the drive over didn't take long.

I'd popped a pill before I left Kisha's crib to help calm my nerves 'cause I didn't know what I was gone say when I got there. By the time I pulled up the street from Nivea's apartment, it had taken effect and mixed with the Remy, a nigga was on cloud nine. I made my way down the block, glad to see that them kids wasn't out there when I got to her building. I texted her as soon as I stopped in front of her door, and then waited on a notification for her texting me back. When five minutes passed, and I still hadn't heard from her, I started ringing her bell repeatedly, not giving a fuck about who I woke up. I needed to get to know the kids anyway, right?

I was still leaning on the doorbell when I saw her coming down the stairs through the glass. She had her hair tied up in a scarf, and that ugly ass robe on again. My jaw clenched knowing that she probably ain't have shit on under it but some little ass shorts.

"What do you want, Judah?" Nivea asked, only opening the door enough to stick her head through like that would keep me out.

"Why you come out here in that lil ass robe?" I frowned, ignoring her question and pushing my way in. Her sweet scent hit me as we stood damn near chest to chest in the small hallway, making me want to bury my face in her neck. She rolled her eyes and tied the robe tighter around herself.

"Well, I wouldn't even be awake if somebody wasn't ringing my bell like he was crazy. For real though, what you want, Ju?" She asked again.

"I want you, that's why I'm here."

She smacked her lips and hit me with a 'boy please' look. "Oh, you want me now, right? Cause the last time you were over here, you didn't. Then I didn't even hear from you and now all of a sudden you're at my door at damn near 2 o'clock in the morning." She was trying to come off angry like she didn't care, but I could see it in her eyes that she was hurt. That night I had dipped out on her, I wasn't really thinking about her feelings and shit. The only thing that had been on my mind was getting the fuck out of dodge. Normally, a female's hurt feelings wasn't my problem, but I could already see that with Nivea things were going to be different.

"I apologize, a'ight?" I said, eliminating the space between us. She tried to back away but there was nowhere for her to run in the cramped hallway.

I was tired of letting shit get between us. At this point, I ain't really care about how old she was or her kids. Shit, I ain't care about either one of her bitch ass baby daddies. I just wanted her, and I was going to have her. I grabbed her waist and drew her body into mine, unmoved by the small amount of resistance she gave me. No matter what Nivea said, she wanted me just as much as I wanted her. It was all in her face, and the way her body melted from my touch. "I was trippin' then bout shit that don't even matter. I just wanna make it right. I just want you to be mine." Shorty had me out here sounding soft as hell.

She shook her head in denial like she wasn't trying to hear that shit though. "You don't know what you want.

Young ass," Nivea scoffed and tried to wiggle away from me, but I wasn't having that. My grip on her tightened, giving her even less room to move as I brought my face closer to hers.

"I do. I want the same thing you want, Nivea. Stop fighting so damn hard and let a nigga have you," I pleaded against her lips. "Just let me have you, a'ight?"

She didn't say anything, but she didn't have to. The way she locked her arms behind my neck and deepened the kiss told me everything I needed to know. My hands roamed the thickness of her body and landed on her round ass, giving it a squeeze. Her soft moaning had my dick straining to get out as she grinded against me and her breathing quickened.

"Come on, let's go upstairs, ma," I whispered, breaking my lips away from hers. She nodded quickly, looking all disheveled and shit. Knowing I had her all excited from a kiss had my head bigger than normal. I grinned cockily and bit into my lip as I followed her up the stairs. Once we reached the landing, I was right back on her, planting kisses on her neck and shoulders. She quickly got the door open and turned around to embrace me as soon as we were inside.

"Where yo kids at?" I questioned, backing her into a hallway that led to her bedroom.

"At their grandma's. Why?" She moaned with her lips still pressed to mine.

"I ain't want you to wake them up with all the screamin' you 'bouta do." I untied her robe and let it fall to the floor as we made it to her bed. I didn't miss the surprised look on her face. Shorty was in for a long night, and she ain't even know it.

The street lights illuminated her room letting me see that she'd only had on some spandex type shorts and a tank top. "Come up out this shit," I said, lifting her tank. She raised her arms to help me take it off and once it hit the floor, I relieved her of the shorts she was wearing. I palmed her pussy, slipping two fingers inside and she whimpered. Her shit was wetter than the ocean and I swear I was ready to drown. I watched in awe as pleasure took over her face. Even with her hair all tied up, she looked gorgeous.

"Can I taste you, ma?" I brought my lips close to her ear and asked before licking her lobe. She clenched around my fingers and squeezed her legs together as she came. With my hand still covered in her juices, I lifted her onto the bed, smoothly pulling away her scarf and letting her hair free. It spread around her head as she laid there like she was supposed to model. I looked down at her fine ass and slipped out of my clothes before hovering over her and brushing my hand across her cheek. "Nivea, can I taste that juicy shit, or nah?"

She opened her eyes slowly and stared back at me for a second before nodding. That was all I needed to see. I had only ever eaten pussy once time in my life, and that was years ago. Only one other female had made me want to please her like that, but something about Nivea made me want to go that extra mile for her. The way she soaked my hand up, I needed to taste her. I didn't break eye contact as I kissed my way down her body, giving special attention to the inside of her thighs. Her scent pulled me in, and I took my time snaking my tongue up her slit. I wasn't even sure of what I was doing, but it must have been right because she was arching her back and chanting my name. When I sucked her clit into my mouth, she rubbed the back of my head softly and grinded her hips.

"Oh shit, Judah!" She groaned breathlessly. She was saying my name sexy as hell and it only made me go harder. I grabbed her thick thighs and pulled her body closer, flicking my tongue rapidly. It was over after that. She started shaking as another orgasm rocked her body and her sweet cream filled my mouth. I licked her clean and planted a kiss on the inside of her thigh before wiping my mouth and grabbing a condom from my jeans. Nivea was on her side with her legs closed, looking like she was ready to fall asleep already.

"I know my young ass ain't tapped you out, Nivea?" I smirked and as I slipped on the condom. She turned over and covered her face with her hands, embarrassed.

"It's been a long time, Judah," she whined.

"So, you done now?" I cocked a brow and covered her body with mine, moving her hands. Her face split into a shy smile as she shook her head.

"Nope, I just need a second."

"Good, 'cause I ain't done with you. I ain't even made you scream yet," I mused, wrapping her legs around my back. "Put it in, baby." I kissed her.

"You so damn cocky." She noted. Once she had her soft hands around my shaft, her eyes widened at my size.

"Now you see why." I grinned down at her and pushed myself between her silky folds slowly. She squeezed her eyes closed tightly and tried to brace herself. "Nivea, relax man. I ain't gone hurt you." She nodded and her eyes fluttered open. I sucked her lip into my mouth, biting it softly as I brought myself fully inside of her.

"Mmmmh, Judahhhhh!" She cried out, tossing her head to the side. I put my face into her neck to stop myself from moaning like a bitch. Nivea was super wet and tight as hell. I put one of her legs in the crook of my arm and dug deeper.

"This my pussy now, Nivea. Understand?" I grunted into her neck and she nodded. Her mouth hung open, only letting out a light moan. "Say it!" I demanded as I continued to drill her.

"Ahhhhh, fuck, Judah! It's yours!"

"Say that shit louder. I want the whole block to know, shorty!"

"Yesssssss, it's yours! It's yours!" She screamed. I couldn't help the smirk that came over my face. I didn't know if she knew it or not, but I wasn't playing and just talking shit. She was mine from the moment I felt this tight ass pussy.

"Glad you know, baby. Now turn over and toot that ass for daddy."

KISHA

I sat outside of the building that Ju had gone into with tears streaming down my face. He had real life left my bed to come over here with this bitch. He didn't even know that I had followed him over here as soon as he left. Shit, I still had on the lingerie because I didn't have time to put on clothes. He probably didn't even care. That's why he had did all that shit with her in the hallway. Out of all the time we had been fucking around, he had never looked at me the way he was in there looking at her. Hell, he had never even kissed me on the mouth, but he was out here just putting his lips on that hoe like they were a real couple. When they went upstairs, I already knew that he was about to give her my dick. I wondered if he was gone wash my slob off it before he fucked her. I could bet his ass ain't tell her he was with me trying to fuck before he came here. *Nasty bitch!* I thought, frowning at the thought.

Even though I knew I was supposed to be mad at Ju, I saw this as that bitch's fault. In my mind, she was the one who came in and ruined everything. Ju might have been telling me that he didn't want to settle down, but his actions were starting to prove otherwise. He had stayed the night and was actually spending time at my house. If I called him and needed something, he took care of it for me. Those were the signs of a man catching feelings if you asked me. Then all of a sudden, this bitch Nivea pops up out of nowhere and snatches him away after all the hard work I had put in. I had been trying for months to prove to him that I was his ride or die, doing shit that I would have never done for anybody else, not even my baby father.

Yeah, I had two kids, but Ju didn't need to know that. I had lost custody of them years ago, so it didn't matter anyway. I'd planned on us starting our own family soon. It wasn't like the little bitches liked me anyway. Whenever their daddy, Montrell, used to leave me alone with them, they would cry the whole time he was gone, which made them get their asses choked, smacked or worse. Apparently, discipline in your own home was wrong. As soon as Trell found out about what I was doing, he took them away, but he just didn't know that he was doing me a favor. I couldn't stand them little hoes anyway, and I didn't think that Ju would want them either. But if a baby mama was the type of bitch he wanted, I could be that too. I had been had kids. If that was the reason why he didn't want me, then I would get them back. That wasn't going to be hard to do. First, I just needed to figure out a way to get rid of this bitch. She didn't even look like she belonged in the hood, so I knew that her ass couldn't fight. It was obvious she was a weak ass bitch, and Ju didn't need no weak hoe on his arm. She was probably just looking for a come up trying to fuck with him. I mean, what thirty-year old woman with all them damn kids would want a twenty-one-year old nigga?

"Old cradle robbin' ass bitc,." I grumbled to myself as I looked up at the building and tried to figure out which crib was hers. I just knew he was up there giving her the bomb ass dick that I was supposed to have been riding. As much as it pained me to know that, I wasn't going to trip. Ju had fucked plenty of bitches while he was fucking me, but I never felt threatened by them because I knew that none of them would last as long as me. This Nivea bitch though, she had to go, and I was gonna die trying to get her and them little bastards out of the picture.

First order of business would be to let her know that me and him were together. I might even whoop her ass too. Then once she no longer wanted to deal with him, I would be right there to help him get over her. Me and my kids. I pulled away from her building and wiped my tears with those plans in mind. It wouldn't be long before Ju left that black bitch alone and got back with me.

NIVEA

*T*he next morning, I woke up stiff and sore as hell to Judah's loud ass in my kitchen listening to rap. I laid there for a minute trying not to smile at how good I felt, but it was no way to hide the 'good dick glow' I was sporting. It had been a long ass time since I had gotten some, and I swear those dreams hadn't prepared me for the shit that Judah had done to my body. I could still feel him between my legs and my pussy throbbed just thinking about all the orgasms I had. I tried to sit up and couldn't. I was definitely going to have to soak in some damn Epsom salt before I went to get the kids.

"Yo' ass gone just lay up in here smiling and shit, or you gone come eat this food a nigga made for you?"

Judah stood leaning against the doorway shirtless, watching me with the corners of his mouth curved up into a grin. I rolled my eyes at him playfully and blushed. "I was not laying here smilin'," I lied, cheesing the whole time. He came further into the room and looked down at me, rubbing a hand across his jaw.

"You can't get up, huh?" He asked, reading my ass, and I couldn't do shit but laugh with him.

"Shut up and help me, Judah." I fake pouted and tried again to sit up unsuccessfully. Everything hurt, but it was a good hurt. One that I hadn't ever had.

"Come on, man," he huffed, holding out his arms for me to grab ahold of. When my hands were in his, he pulled me up on my feet and slipped his big ass shirt over my head. "Look at yo' ass lookin' all freshly fucked," he teased, giving me a kiss.

"Whateva, you swear you did somethin'." I waved him off as I went to walk away and had to stop because of how sore my pussy was.

"You can't even walk, shorty. You know I put that thang down." Judah laughed, slapping me hard as hell on the ass and walking out of the room. "Hurry up! Yo' food gon' be cold!" He yelled over his shoulder.

It took me a second, but I waddled into the kitchen after brushing my teeth to find him already at the table eating a plate of pancakes, eggs and bacon. I couldn't deny that I was surprised his little ass even knew how to cook. He looked up from his plate and pointed to where mine was sitting on the table right across from his. "Took yo' ass long enough. I had to put that shit in the microwave like twice," he complained.

"Well, it ain't like my legs functioning properly, Judah," I said, sitting at the table and taking a small bite of the eggs. Nothing smelled or looked burnt, but that ain't mean nothing. I'd seen people mess up cooking small shit like eggs before, and I wasn't trying to throw up nothing.

"That's that young ass dick for you," he boasted, flashing a grin. I flipped his ass the bird with one hand and shoveled more food into my mouth with the other. It was actually good. I couldn't even front, but the pancakes tasted familiar as hell. I squinted my eyes at him suspiciously as I chewed. "I got you as soon as we finished." He winked.

"Yeah a'ight. You ain't comin' near my pussy," I lied 'cause my body was already wanting him again, but that shit was gone wait. The look he gave me said he was on my body's side.

"Quit playing. I told yo' ass that's my pussy. I wasn't just sayin' that shit." My clit twitched involuntarily, and I had to squeeze my thighs together. She was definitely addicted to Judah's sex.

"Did you cook this?" I asked, ignoring what he'd said. I wasn't about to get into a debate that I knew he was going to win. Last night when he had asked if it was his, I wasn't lying when I told him it was. Besides, I didn't think I would even want anybody else to touch me now that Judah had left his mark.

"Nigga, yeah I cooked. What you think, I can't have skills in the kitchen too?" He said, trying to keep a straight face that instantly told me he was lying. "A'ight, real shit, I ran and got this shit from IHOP, but it's the thought that counts, right?"

"I knew yo' ass ain't really cook," I giggled, covering my mouth since it was still full of food. I must have been hungry as hell because I'd cleaned my plate fast.

"So, you sayin' you don't appreciate my gesture?" He cocked his head at me and licked his lips, reminding me of how he'd feasted on me last night. This nigga was gon' be the death of me, I could already see it. He stood up and came over to stand between my legs, looking like a whole meal with dessert. The look in his eyes let me know exactly what was on his mind.

"Yesss, I appreciate it," I moaned as he dipped his head down into the crook of my neck, working that damn tongue. I forgot what we were even talking about. He slid his hands up my thighs, and I pushed them right back away, shaking him off me.

"I'm not fuckin' with you," I laughed standing up and moving out of his reach. "I told you I'm already sore." Dropping my plate into the sink, I turned around to find Judah right behind me. He looked like he was enjoying my discomfort, knowing that it was because of him.

"I'ma let you make it until later, shorty. Besides, I'm tryna spend the day with you and the kids." He looked down at me expectantly like he wasn't sure of what I would say. I wasn't sure if I was ready for him to meet the kids. Not on no couple shit anyway. We had literally just sort of made things official last night.

There were things I didn't know about him and his lifestyle that could affect my kids. What if he was still in the streets? What if he had a crazy ass baby mama somewhere? It was just too many *what ifs* for me.

"That's sweet, but ummm… are you sure that you're ready for that?" I wanted to know. I didn't want him to try and jump into officially meeting the kids just because he thought that was what I wanted. They already had a father, and even though he was locked away, I didn't need Judah to fill the void. If things continued between us, I wanted him to have a desire to be in the kids' lives, not just be there because he thought he was supposed to. His brows drew together at my question.

"Nah, I ain't ready, but if you're mine and I'm yours then that shit don't matter, right? I'm tryna be there for you, and that includes being there for them. I can't learn if you don't teach me." That had to be some of the sweetest shit I'd ever heard, and I could tell that he was serious, but that still didn't stop me from being skeptical. I'd never been the type to let my kids meet every man that I dealt with. Even Quad didn't meet Kymia right away. And since he had been the only man in their lives, I wondered how they would take Judah.

"That's really sweet, Judah, but I think we should at least see if we will work before throwing my kids in the mix." I feared the look on his face from my response. I just knew his feelings would be hurt or worse, he would get upset. But when our eyes met, he just nodded with a blank expression.

"You right, shorty. Respect. I'ma just follow yo' lead on this."

I smiled widely and pulled him in for a kiss, letting his arms slip around my waist until his phone rang. He tried to ignore it the first time, but after it went off again, he reluctantly answered. Almost immediately his eyes darkened at whatever the other person was saying. I couldn't make out what they were talking about, but I knew it was a man at least.

"A'ight, I'ma come through there," Judah finally spoke after a few seconds, stuffing the phone back down into his pocket.

"Is everything ok?" I asked.

"Yeah, everything straight. I just gotta go holla at my nigga Pree right quick." He gave me a quick kiss and then headed out of the kitchen without waiting on a reply. He came back a second later with his hoodie and gym shoes on. "I'ma call you later, a'ight?"

He gave me one last kiss and then he was gone. I heard the front door slam behind him and figured I'd better get my ass up and get ready to get the kids. They had already been at Brenda's house too long. She would definitely call me soon, telling me to come get their bad asses and I liked to beat her to the punch. Brenda wasn't all that bad, but she constantly had her hand out thinking that Quad had a secret stash somewhere. And she never wanted to deal with the kids for too long. It had been like five months since the last time she had seen them, and if it wasn't for them asking to go, it probably would have been another five.

I walked to the bathroom gap legged and ran me a super hot bath, making sure to add some epsom salt to the water. I didn't even wait for the tub to fill up before I sat my sore ass down in it and let out a sigh of relief. After soaking, I drained the water and cut on the shower so that I could wash up, being extra careful with my sensitive private area.

Twenty minutes later, I was dressed down in some black leggings, and a plain white tank with a blue jean top over it. I'd called Niyah to come pick me up, but she was busy, so I guess the bus was going to be my transportation for the day. My phone chirped with a notification, and I saw that Judah had messaged me. I couldn't help the smile that covered my face just that quick. I needed to get my shit together and fast. Judah hadn't even been around long enough to have me feeling all mushy inside. Yet, here I was, smiling and feeling butterflies over a text. I opened the message as I slipped my feet into a pair of black flats.

Judah: I got a surprise for you outside. See you later, beautiful.

Me: What did you do, Judah?

Judah: Man, just take yo' ass outside

He didn't have to tell me twice. I grabbed my purse and keys and made my way down the stairs to see this surprise of his. My mouth fell open in shock when I saw my car parked right out front. I snatched the glass door open and ran out to make sure it was really my baby. I could see Quad's car seat, and Quina's booster through the window. Judah had went and gotten my car for me. I swear I almost broke down crying, I was so happy. The repairs had been way too much for me and after losing my job, I thought it would take forever to get it back. I circled it and admired the good job they'd done. You couldn't even tell that it was in an accident at all. The front bumper looked brand new and the paint was sparkling like it was freshly done. I pulled my phone out to call and thank Judah for doing this for me, but his voicemail picked up, so I just left a message. A call from Quad came through before I could put my phone away, and I just sat staring.

Seeing the prison number flash across my screen instantly brought my mood straight down. The last time I'd talked to Quad was when I told him I was still rocking with him, and I'd just turned around and let Judah stake a claim on me. Guilt filled me, and I ignored the call, hoping he wouldn't call me right back thinking that I was sleeping or something. I needed time to think before I talked to him. I needed to know for sure if me and Judah even stood a chance.

Although I felt like this thing between us was real, the fact of the matter was that Judah may change his mind about what he wanted. He was young, way younger than me by my standards and a rapper. There weren't very many rappers these days that had girlfriends. And if they did have them, they didn't claim them. I didn't know if I was ready to live the life of a famous nigga's woman and be under all types of microscopes.

This was too much to be thinking about so early in the morning, especially when I was still dick dizzy from the long night I'd had with Judah. That was definitely going to cause me problems considering that it was still heavily on my mind. I rejected another call from Quad's persistent ass and jumped in my car, rubbing the steering wheel and dash like it was a real person.

"Hey baby," I gushed, smiling so hard my cheeks hurt. "I missed you."

This was another reason why I was leaning more towards Judah. Ever since I'd met him, he had been looking out for me with no questions asked and so far with no expectations. Despite the obvious age difference and his chosen career, there wasn't nothing wrong with him. Like Niyah had said, I deserved to be happy and right now, Judah made me happy. I just needed to get out of my own way.

I pulled up to Quad's mama house thirty minutes later and saw the kids outside playing in the yard while Kymia sat on the porch, eyes glued to that damn phone. As soon as QJ saw me, he started screaming my name and so did Quiana. I guess Brenda must have heard the commotion because she came out onto the porch as soon as my foot touched the street. I could tell she had an attitude already and it wasn't because her hair dresser had dyed her shit a bright orange and red color. Brenda swore she was in her teens the way she dressed. Today she had on some hot pink capris with a white crop top displaying her pierced belly button. A thick cloud of smoke trailed behind her from the Newport she had dangling out of her mouth. I was surprised it wasn't a blunt. Brenda smoked and kicked it like she wasn't a forty something year old woman. I made it around to the sidewalk where the kids were standing waiting to jump on me.

"Girl, you late as hell! How you know I ain't have shit to do today?" Brenda snapped once I was within a foot of the porch. "I hope you wasn't out here thottin' while my SON in jail! He already told me you was ignoring his calls today!" My mouth fell open at the crazy shit she was spewing. *No this old bitch ain't talkin' 'bout thottin!* I thought to myself. I wondered if it was that obvious that Judah had fucked the soul out of my body. My cheeks flushed thinking about it, but I still lied.

"It's not even 11 yet, Brenda, and wasn't nobody out here doin' shit. I was home getting some sleep."

"Ummmhmm, well why didn't you answer the phone for Quad?" She asked, cutting me off and flicking her ash in the bushes next to us.

"Because I was getting my car and talking to the mechanic." The lie came out easily. She gave me one of them looks that said she ain't believe shit I was saying, and then looked from my car back to me.

"How you get that piece of shit fixed anyway? Last I checked, you ain't have no money. I knew Quad's ass left somethin'," she grumbled, frowning up her face.

"I got a better payin' job, Brenda, and my boss gave me an advance to get it fixed, so I wouldn't have to keep taking the kids on the bus." I hated that I felt the need to explain myself to her of all people. She never offered me or the kids a ride, and she had a damn car sitting right in her driveway.

"Right." She quipped, staring at me like she could see through my lies. "Y'all go get y'all shit so you can go." She nodded her head towards the house and the kids all went inside. As soon as the screen slammed behind them, she bent down a little, so she was closer to me.

"I don't know who you think you foolin', Nivea, but I ain't new to this shit, I'm true to it. I done heard about you being seen with some lil rap nigga while my son in jail." I went to interrupt, but she put a hand up to stop me. "I ain't tryna hear no lies from up outta you. I know it's true just from the look on yo' face but let me tell you this. Don't get caught up like my son won't be here one of these days." She gave me a pointed look just as the kids rushed back out with their bags. I wasn't about to argue with her crazy ass today, especially about Quad when she was barely even there for him. She was a damn fool if she thought that Quad was about to be getting out anytime soon and an even bigger fool if she thought I was gone tell her big mouth ass shit.

I pointed for the kids to go ahead to the car and brought my attention back to Brenda. "I don't know what you think you know, Brenda, but I got this, ok? You have a good day." I hadn't even turned around good when her cellphone rang, and a grin covered her face.

"Yeah, Quad, she right here," she said, shoving her phone into my hand.

"Yo' why the fuck ain't you answerin' the phone man?" He barked in my ear.

"I was busy, Quad, damn!" I was beyond irritated that this old bitch had just tried me like this. I turned my back to her for a little bit more privacy even though I knew her ass was still tuned into everything coming out of both our mouths. Don't ask me how.

"Oh, you yellin' at a nigga now? You actin' real funny right now, Nivea." I could hear the frown in his voice, and I wondered if maybe I was acting funny. Was I on some other shit because of Judah or was it because I was tired of the prison wife role? I took a deep breath to try and get my attitude under control.

"I'm not yellin', Quad. It's just that I was doing something when you called and it's kinda fucked up that as soon as I'm unavailable, you and yo' mama automatically assume that I'm on some funny shit." I turned around and rolled my eyes at Brenda who was still standing there all in my mouth.

"My bad, bae, but you know how I be when I don't talk to you. Then my OG talkin' bout you fuckin' with Ju Savage and shit. What I'm supposed to think?" My eyes met Brenda's when he said that. Of course, that bitch had went out of her way to inform him about Judah. It was like she lived for drama with her over grown ass. "What the fuck was you doing leaving the club with him, Nivea? How you even know that lil nigga?"

"I don't know him, ok! I went out to celebrate passing my finals, and Ky was there tryna get in my face talkin' crazy. Judah just helped me is all."

"Judah, huh? It seems like it's more to it than you sayin'. It sounds like y'all a lil personal. Are you fuckin' his young ass? Who else you done fucked? Ky? That's why he was in yo' face and shit!" He roared loudly. I pulled the phone away from my ear and looked at it because he was truly trying to go off on me when I'd just told him what happened.

"I'm not 'bouta listen to this shit from you, Quad. I ain't did nothin' to make you question me! You and yo' mama can sit over here and talk about what y'all think y'all know, and I'ma go home and take care of my kids like I been doin'." I held the phone out to Brenda and ignored the yelling I could hear coming from Quad.

I did feel a small bit of guilt about fucking Judah, but him accusing me of fucking Ky and basically calling me a hoe erased that feeling quick. He knew how I felt about Ky, so he was just speaking out of anger, unless he really thought I would do some shit like that. I know men in jail were insecure about shit because they weren't around, but I was taught that niggas only accuse you of shit that their doing. Just because I hadn't answered the phone, this nigga automatically assumed I was fucking around, and his raggedy ass mama wasn't making it any better.

I barely waited for her to get the phone in her hand good before I walked away. The way I was feeling right now, I wished the shit would have fallen and cracked. She must have caught it though because I could hear her talking shit right along with Quad as I made it to the car.

"Ma, when you get the car back?" Quiana's little nosy self asked once I got inside.

"Today." Was all I said because I was too pissed off to go into detail with her. I'm sure she could tell too because she didn't ask anymore questions like she usually did. I decided not to even go home. After witnessing that stupid shit back there, I wanted the kids to have fun and I needed something to take my mind off of Quad and his mama. It took me almost an hour to get to Chuck E Cheese. As soon as we pulled up, Kymia's attitude reared its ugly head.

"Ugh, ma! I don't wanna play this baby stuff," she whined, smacking her lips and shit while her brother and sister cheered from the backseat.

"Well, this is where we goin', so fix yo' face and let's go."

I wasn't in the mood for her shit today. Her best bet was to leave me alone right now. I took a moment to glance at my phone as I got out and Judah still hadn't called or messaged me. That was also contributing to my bad mood. I wasn't sure how this whole thing was supposed to work, but I didn't like feeling ignored. I tried to call him again and this time it went straight to voicemail. Shaking my head, I helped QJ out the car and held his hand as we all walked in with Kymia taking her sweet ass time behind us. I paid for our tokens and some pizza and took a seat at one of the tables, glad that it wasn't packed full of people.

Since it was gone be a while for the pizza, I gave Quiana a cup of tokens for her and I carried the other one for QJ. She ran off ahead of us and started playing one of those games that gave you tickets for nothing while QJ pulled me towards the car game. He loved cars, so this was right up his alley. I sat him in my lap and put in the two tokens it took to play. We played three games with me steady crashing. I had never been good at driving games, but he didn't even notice. He caught sight of a game with guns and hopped his little bad ass off me and ran there next.

"Mama, I wanna shoot," he said, pointing. Of course, he couldn't reach this one either, but there wasn't a seat, so I had to pick him up. I put in the tokens for him and hoisted him up, so he could shoot some zombies. "I'm killin' 'em, ma!" He told me as he shot aimlessly at the screen.

"Ooooh, you killin' all of 'em, QJ! Daannnnng!" I exaggerated cause his ass wasn't killing nothing. I was wondering if maybe I should get him a game like he'd been asking for. He was doing much better than I expected. When the game was over, he was still trying to shoot at the screen. "You tryna play again?"

"Yeah!" He shouted and busted out dancing as I put more coins in. He was so silly, but I loved it. Quiana came over right then with a handful of tickets.

"I wanna play with QJ, ma," she said, trying to hand me her tickets.

"Girl, you can play, but I can't hold yo' tickets and him, so you either gone have to put them in yo' pocket or take them to the table." She stood there for a second trying to contemplate whether or not she felt like going all the way back to the table before stuffing them into the pocket of her jean shorts and putting in her two coins to play.

"Now me and QJ 'bouta whoop you real quick, so we can go eat. Ain't that right, Qj?"

"Yep!" He nodded hard as I picked him up again. We played three games with Quiana before I finally got too tired to hold him anymore.

"Come on, y'all. I'm tired and hungry," I sighed, setting QJ down on his feet. "We whooped yo' tail enough for now, Quiana."

"You was helpin' QJ, ma. That don't even count." Quiana stood there pouting with her arms folded. I swear my kids had to be some of the sorest losers when it came to games. It didn't matter what it was, it was always somebody else's fault if they lost.

"Awwww, it's okay, baby. Next time we play something, I'll help you," I cooed, putting an arm around her shoulder and pulling her along with us. That seemed to do the trick because she was in a much better mood by the time we got back to the table with Kymia. The pizza had already been brought over and she'd started eating some. I gave QJ four pieces and grabbed two for myself.

"Ma, we had fun at Grandma Brenda house! Uncle Jay was there, and he let us play his game!" Quiana told me around a mouthful of pizza.

I narrowed my eyes in irritation. Brenda ass knew I didn't like Jay's twisted ass around my damn kids. He always rubbed me the wrong way, not to mention he was always into some shit with Quad but never got caught. I looked to Kymia for confirmation even though Quiana never lied, and she gave me an uninterested shrug. Now I was pissed at Brenda's ugly ass all over again. I'd already made it up in my mind that my kids weren't going back over there no more. It was no telling what Jay's dumb ass had going on, and I didn't want my kids involved. We stayed a few more hours before I dragged them all home. Despite the day's drama, they had fun and I had even got Kymia to play a few games before we left. Now all I had to do was talk to Judah, but that was seeming easier said than done since he still hadn't called me. I wasn't trying to seem clingy already, so I stopped trying to get in touch with him and just chilled with my kids. I would definitely see him at some point.

SAVAGE

When Pree had hit me up, it was to say that he
had a location on Keys from The Goon Squad.
It wasn't exactly who I wanted, but he was close enough. Jay
was turning out to be way slicker than I had assumed. All he
had was niggas he ran with. No family, no kids, and no girlfriends that I could find. Anybody I talked to about him
either wasn't giving him up or real life didn't know shit
about him. I was positive that Keys would tell me something
though; either that or he was gone get his shit split. I'd
stopped off on the way and had Mone drop off Nivea's car to
her crib. It had been sitting in his garage for a couple days
because I'd been too busy and too in my feelings to drop it
off. When I figured that he had had enough time to drive
over there, I shot her a text to go look outside. I wished I
could have been there to see the look on her face when she
saw it, but I had some more important shit to take care of at
the moment.

I pulled up to the carwash that Pree told me he was at and
saw that nigga right away. He was so busy cheesing in some
hoe's face that he ain't even see me. I shook my head at his

little dumb ass and approached him as soon as shorty switched off trying to shake her ass extra hard. It was doing the trick too cause that niggas eyes were locked until I stepped into his line of vision. He instantly froze up and tried to back away, but there was nowhere for him to run since his car was right behind him. Realizing this, he let out a nervous laugh.

"What's up, Savage?"

"Wassup, Keys," I said, grinning with my gun down by my side. You a hard lil nigga to find, you know that?"

"Man, I ain't have shit to do with that. I barely even know the nigga Jay," he stammered, flinching away. He looked like he was about to shit himself, and I hadn't even pointed the gun at him yet. This was the type of nigga they wanted to be the face of Chicago?

"Right, so tell me what you do know," I demanded, ready to crack his ass the minute I felt like he was lying.

"I just said I barely know his ass, man," he whined, and I hit his ass right across his shit with the butt of my gun. It started leaking blood down his face, and he let out a shriek. "What the fuck man! We got a photo shoot in the mornin'!" He cried between his fingers.

"You sound like a bitch *we gotta photo shoot in the morning* ass nigga," I mocked. "Tell me what the fuck I wanna know or I'ma hit you with more than just these hands."

"A'ight, a'ight." He threw his hands up in surrender. "I ain't even heard from dude since that shit happened with Trigga. We just know him from around the way man. He got an older brother, but that nigga in jail. He might be at his mama crib tho."

"You know where that bitch live?"

"Yeah, she stays over on Halsted." He groaned and pointed like we could see straight to her house or something.

"Nigga, do I look like I can see her house from here?" I questioned through my teeth. "Take me over there."

"Ok, man, ok." He went to walk around to the driver's side of his car still holding his nose, and I yanked his ass right back.

"Yo' ass ain't drivin', nigga." I pushed him towards my car and waited while he got in on the passenger side. Once he closed the door, I got in behind him with my gun sitting on my lap, so his ass knew not to try no funny shit. A call came through from Nivea's fine ass, but I had to hit ignore. I know she was excited about having her car back and shit, but I would have to get up with her later. I looked over at Keys' scary ass all stuffed against the door. "Put yo' damn seat belt on." He looked like he wanted to try and get me pulled over for some dumb shit like that. I sped off as soon as I heard the seatbelt click and made each turn that he told me to until we pulled up in front of her house.

I was surprised as fuck to see Nivea out there going back and forth with some old bitch. I was about to light her ass up too until I saw her three kids walking out with book bags. "Who is she to Jay?" I questioned.

"That's his brother's baby mama," was all he said.

"That nigga's brother is snitchin' ass Quad?" I never would have known that from looking. They didn't look shit alike, and nobody had mentioned him. I could understand that shit though 'cause if I was that nigga, I wouldn't want nobody associating me with a snitch as my blood.

"Yeah, he don't like people knowing about Quad tho," Keys said aloud exactly what I'd been thinking. "That's his OG she arguin' with; that broad swear she 'bout the life." I broke my gaze away from the scene that Nivea and dude mama was making to look at his ass. He was sitting in the car giving me details about a nigga he fucked with and had the nerve to talk about some street life shit. The skinny jeans I kept seeing his ass in had me questioning his gangsta, but this rat shit let me know he wasn't who he claimed to be. I didn't even say shit. I just tuned back in to their conversation, hearing my name pop up repeatedly.

Nivea ain't tell me shit about still messing with her bitch ass baby daddy. If I was being mature and level headed about it, I would admit that I hadn't really gave her time to tell me shit. But I wasn't level headed, and I ain't feel like being mature right now. I sat flexing my fingers around the steering wheel while she went back and forth on the phone with who I'm assuming was Quad and fought the urge to pop right up on her. Evidently, I was already the topic of conversation, but I wasn't here for Nivea. And I wasn't trying to fuck up my chance to get at that nigga Jay over some pussy. I would deal with Nivea's ass later.

She didn't stay on the phone arguing for long before she handed it back to dude mama and walked off. I waited until she got into her car and pulled away before addressing Keys with my eyes still glued to the porch. "A'ight, get yo lil snitch ass on!" I spat, nodding my head toward the door.

As an afterthought, I snatched him back and put my gun in his face. "It goes without saying that this shit right here gon' be kept between us, right?" Keys' eyes bucked and he nodded hard with his scary ass.

"Ye-Yeah, bro. I won't say shit!" He squeaked, irritating me. I let him go for now, knowing that I would have to get up with him sooner rather than later. If his ass would snitch on his homie, I know he'd snitch on me. I watched him disappear around the corner, then dialed up Pree.

"Wassup, youngin'? Did that nigga have anything of use for you?" He cut straight to the point.

"Hell yeah, he told me a lot, but I'ma put you on in a sec. What's yo' location?" I asked, glancing back at the porch to see Jay's mama finally going inside.

"I just left the hospital, on my way to the stu."

"Oh yeah, how my nigga doin'?" I wanted to know. I hadn't been back up to the hospital since Pree pulled me out that day. It didn't feel right going up there when I hadn't made any strides in finding the nigga that had put him there. Besides that, it was hard as fuck to see him like that, hooked up to all types of machines and shit.

"Still the same. Jackie was up there too." I frowned at the way he said my OG name. Like his ass was familiar with her, but I shook that thought quick. My mama wouldn't fuck with a nigga like Pree. That much I was certain of.

"A'ight, I'm 'bouta meet you there my nigga."

"Bet."

I hung up and pulled my car away from the curb, applying the address to memory. I was coming back, and I was going to wait Jay's ass out. It didn't matter what a nigga was running from, he would always check in with his OG, so it was only a matter of time before he brought his ass around. And as soon as he did, I was gone lay his ass down. A nigga might even kill his mama too just because. I mused as I pulled up to a red light. My phone buzzed with another call from Nivea, and I hit ignore before going ahead and cutting that shit off. I didn't have time to deal with her right now. For one, she was distracting as fuck, had me thinking about shit like waking up to her, spending time with her and the kids. Shit I didn't have time to think about right now. Plus, I was feeling some type of way about her being with her baby daddy. Just because his ass was locked up didn't mean shit to me. Technically, they were still together. Add to that the fact that she denied me to him and his mama like I was some type of fucking side nigga. She was used to dealing with niggas like Quad and Ky, so she thought shit like this was cool. It wasn't. And I was gone be the one to teach her ass that as soon as I took care of Jay.

After meeting Pree at the studio, I went home to shower since I didn't get a chance to at Nivea's. I sat on my couch in a beater and some hoopin' shorts with my guns laid out on the table in front of me. It was hard to decide which one I was gon' use, but since Jay's death was gon' be special, I went ahead and loaded up my twin, gold plated desert eagles. I wasn't sure how long it would take to get him to his mama's crib, but I was willing to wait him out.

The sound of somebody banging at my door had me on my feet with a gun down at my side. I had already talked to Pree and my OG that day. Nobody else even knew where I lived besides Mone. I checked the peephole and got irritated as fuck at the sight of Kisha standing in front of my door in some grey Nike shorts, and a plain white fitted tshirt. I pinched the bridge of my nose and released a deep sigh. Something told me not to open the door, but of course I ain't listen.

"How the fuck you know where I live yo'?" I snapped, snatching the door open. She looked scared for a second but got herself together quick and gave me a seductive smile.

"I got yo' address from Pree, Ju. I just wanted to check on you and make sure you were ok," she said, trying to step around me, but I blocked her quick.

"I'm fine. Beat it." I started to shut the door on her, but she got in the way and looked up at me sincerely.

"I know you're not fine, Judah." I mugged her hard for saying my name like I allowed that, and she fixed that shit quick. "I mean, Ju. You need a friend. Let me be that." Her voice got low and she moved closer, pushing her body into me.

I wanted to tell her silly ass I ain't need no friends, that my friend was laid up in the damn hospital, but I let her in anyway. She walked further inside, looking around and touching shit before she spun around to face me.

"Are you hungry? I can cook you something real quick," she said casually, and I realized that I hadn't ate shit since breakfast.

"Yo' ass don't know how to cook." I laughed, moving past her and plopping down on the couch. I hadn't seen shorty cook shit besides a noodle cup at the studio since I met her, and she thought she was gone burn my kitchen down. She smacked her lips, and chuckled.

"Boy, you got me fucked up, I can definitely burn."

"Yeah, burn my kitchen to the ground," I cracked.

"Omg! Ju, is you hungry or not? I ain't 'bouta keep letting you go in on my skills." She folded her arms across her chest and shook her head. "Can't even be nice to niggas."

"Gone head then lil Betty Crocker, but real shit, if you burn somethin', you payin' for it." I told her, getting comfortable and cutting on the tv. I ain't know what she was gone find back there 'cause I really ain't cook shit either besides cereal and noodles, but my OG always made sure my fridge was stocked.

"Ain't nobody gon burn shit," she grumbled, walking away from me in search of the kitchen.

Like a half hour later, my crib was smelling good as fuck and my stomach rumbled. I could hear her moving around and shit like she really knew what she was doing as she sang along to that *Boo'd up* shit. "See, I can cook," she said, coming around the corner with two plates in her hand. She sat one down on the coffee table, not at all moved by the guns that were still there and took a seat beside me.

"Nigga, you made some hamburger helper?" I chuckled.

"What's wrong with hamburger helper?" She looked at me with her head tilted.

"Nothin' if you feedin' a toddler. What the fuck I'ma do with this shit? I'ma grown ass man. You ain't even put no chicken or shit on the side."

"I said I can cook, boy, I ain't say what. And hamburger helper is a full meal, you don't need no chicken, greedy ass. Ain't even tasted it and you complaining already." She pouted and took a bite of hers.

"You lucky I'm hungry as fuck," I told her, poking one of the noodles with my fork and easing it into my mouth. I was scared as fuck to eat that shit for real, but she had already eaten half hers. That didn't mean it tasted good though; she had probably gotten used to her bad cooking.

"Boy, don't play with me. It's good." She ate another forkful and rolled her eyes. The small piece that I'd tasted wasn't so bad, but I was still nervous as fuck to take a full bite. She watched me as I loaded up my fork and put it to my mouth like she was anxious about what I would think. I said a quick prayer and ate it, surprised that she hadn't fucked it up, even though it was hard to fuck up something like hamburger helper.

"See." She grinned happily after I went to eat more.

"Nigga, my lil sister can cook this," I teased, eating some more.

"Whateva," she said, sucking her teeth.

We sat there chilling for a minute, and I even ate another plate. Kisha was acting cool as hell, and I wondered why I hadn't just tried to kick it with her outside of fucking or the studio. My eyes started feeling heavy as fuck. I tried to fight that shit though because I ain't care how cool Kisha was acting, I wasn't about to let her be there while I was sleep. "Aye ma, you need to go. I'm tired as fuck," was the last thing I remembered saying before sleep took over.

KISHA

$\mathcal{I}$ waited until I heard light snores coming from Ju before I got the courage to move. Me cooking for him and putting an x pill and sleep aide in it had all been a part of my plan. I had been worried that he wouldn't let me in at all considering how our night had ended the last time we were together, but I was glad that he did. I guess I didn't always have to use my body to get things that I wanted from men. Who knew? Anyway, I didn't have much time, so I searched his pockets for his phone and came up empty. It wasn't anywhere on the couch or the floor, so it had to be in his room. Excitement ran through me at the thought of finally seeing his bedroom. I wished I could have set my scene up in there, but I knew I wouldn't be able to move Ju's heavy ass. That was okay though because the couch would get the job done too.

I checked the first door that was across from the couch and smiled. His room was big and decorated in black. He had rap lyrics spray painted on the wall like a mural over his king-sized bed. The shit was truly ghetto, but it fit him perfectly, and I couldn't lie… it was cute for his bachelor pad. We would have to think of something a bit more female friendly when we moved in together though.

I took a seat on his bed and sank into its plushness. I should have known his shit would be way more comfortable than mine. If I had a bed like this, I wouldn't sleep at a bitch's house either. I fell back into his pillows, enjoying the way his scent surrounded me. I imagined us laying in this bed together, cuddling, fucking, just laying around and writing lyrics. Those thoughts pushed me to hurry up and finish this. I felt around the bed for his phone and found it right next to me. He had it turned off, so I cut it on frowning as it continuously pinged with notifications. I ignored the social media alerts and went straight to the texts that I saw coming in from that bitch Nivea. She had called three times and when he didn't answer, sent back to back texts. I rolled my eyes at how thirsty she seemed, steady blowing his phone up, first asking if he was okay. After that, it was hello, I know you see these type texts. Well, I was here to let her know that Ju was just fine with the woman he was going to be with.

I stood up and shed the clothes I had on, revealing nothing underneath but a lacy, pink thong and bra set. A devilish grin came over my face as I strutted back into the living room where Ju was still knocked out with his head thrown back and straddled his lap. He let out a slight groan when I put my full weight down, but his eyes didn't open. In fact, he wrapped his arms around my slim waist, and pulled me closer. I ignored him mumbling that bitch's name and pulled up the camera on his phone, sending a seductive smirk Nivea's way.

Nivea, as you can see, Judah is just fine. Now can you stop interrupting us *kissing emoji*

I threw my head back and giggled as I imagined the look

on her face when she opened that text. She was gonna be so hurt, but I wasn't done yet. I made sure to post the picture to both his instagram, and facebook with the caption: *Bae*.

The reactions and comments started rolling in almost immediately, and I swear it made me hot as fuck. I grinded myself into his dick that was easily visible through the basketball shorts he wore. It didn't take much for him to rise to the occasion, and I stood up to take my thong off, before climbing back on top of him and setting his beautiful dick free. My mouth watered just looking at it, and I wished I had time to taste him, but I didn't know how long it would be before he woke up.

I lifted myself up to put him inside of me and moaned loudly. Ju had always worn a condom with me, even when he was drunk, he never forgot or slipped up. Now I see it was because he knew I would get addicted for real. My juices ran down his shaft, wetting the top of his shorts as I leaned back and held on to his knees for support. I was throwing this pussy on him so hard that I was coming within minutes. He was murmuring in his sleep and grunting right along with me. I knew he was close to coming when he squeezed my ass real tight and started fucking me back.

"Hmmmmm, shit, Ju!" I cried, speeding up my movements. I sat up so that I could kiss him on the lips one time and was surprised to see his eyes open, staring at me angrily. For a second, I wanted to jump off of him and run, but I realized that he was still fucking me back. He grabbed the back of my hair roughly pulling my head back.

"Ssssss, Kish, take this dick," he said groggily, obviously still feeling the effects of the drugs I'd given him. At least he knew it was me and was hard.

That had me showing out and going harder than before. I was on my porn star shit, and I knew he was gone be sprung after feeling this 'wet wet' without a rubber, just like I was. I felt him pulsing inside me and knew he was about to bless me with his seed. That was until he knocked me clear off of him, and I landed on the floor. I watched as his thick cum erupted and landed on his thigh. I didn't even have time to feel the pain from me landing on his hardwood floors before he pinned me with that same evil glare as before.

"Get the fuck out, Kish," he told me, standing to his feet and pulling his shorts up too.

"What-why? You was just into it, Ju. I thought-"

"You thought coming in here and fuckin' me was gon' change my mind? Bitch, this the exact reason I'm leavin' yo' nutty ass alone!" He barked, making me jump away. He walked towards the back mumbling about how he should have known not to let me in and how crazy I was. He came back a second later mugging me and then his plate that was still sitting on the table empty. "What the fuck you put in that shit!"

"I didn't put nothin' in it, Ju, I swear!" I lied straight through my teeth, clutching my chest. He grabbed one of the guns from his table and walked up on me so fast, I screamed.

"Shut up! Yo ass wasn't screaming when you came in here on that goofy shit!" He pointed his gun under my chin and got close enough that our lips were almost touching. "Stay the fuck away from me, a'ight? I swear I'll kill you Kish and then go lay up with Nivea like ain't shit happen. Stop fuckin' playing with me." Tears fell from my eyes as he stood in my face breathing hard and staring at me like he was considering shooting my ass right here. "Get the fuck outta here, man."

He didn't have to tell me twice. I didn't even attempt to grab my clothes. I just snatched my panties up from the floor and ran until I got to my car. I didn't even care about all the people out there with their phones out recording me. All I could think about was how I almost just died and what he was going to do when he got on Facebook and talked to Nivea. He didn't kill me today, but he was definitely going to once he saw that. I peeled away from his block with only one thing on my mind. Getting the fuck out the city until he calmed down.

NIVEA

I felt stupid. There was really no other way to describe my current state. Not only had that bitch sent me the picture of her and Judah, but she shared that shit all over social media. It wasn't like anybody knew about me and Judah but me, him, Kisha and Niyah. Still, her doing that was disrespectful as fuck. She was sending a clear message to me. It was obvious that Judah had come over here and fucked me just to go back and be with her. No wonder his ass wasn't answering the phone. It was because he had his girlfriend in his lap. What could I say though when we hadn't even had a conversation about whether or not we were both single? Plus, I still hadn't officially ended things with Quad, and now I was glad that I hadn't.

I'd made a fool of myself thinking that there was any way me and a nigga ten years younger than me could be anything other than what we were. I was just an older woman that he got to fuck and as bad as I wanted to dwell on the fact that I'd gotten played, I couldn't. I had kids to raise, bills to pay, and a degree to get. Still, the fact that I was as old as I was, and I'd let his little ass fill me with bullshit was a hard pill to swallow. At my age, I should have saw this shit coming and not let anything he had said get to me. My loneliness had convinced me to give it a try, and that shit had backfired fast.

"Ma! Did you hear what I said?" Quiana asked, interrupting my thoughts. I shook my head and tried to focus on the last thing she'd been talking about before I zoned out, but it was no use. Quina was always talking and jumping from one subject to the next. I couldn't ever keep up with her conversations.

"No, I ain't hear you, baby. What you say?"

"I saaaaaid, don't forget to bring me back some cake?" Our eyes met in the rearview and she gave me the most serious face.

"I know, Quiana, girl," I said, rolling my eyes. The kids were out for summer break and when I dropped them off to my mama's, Quiana had a special request for red velvet cake from the bakery.

"Just making sure 'cause you be forgetting stuff," she quipped, unsnapping her seatbelt as we parked in front of my mama house, and then releasing QJ from his.

"Bye, lil girl." I quickly dismissed her.

"Bye ma!" They both said, slamming the door shut and running into the house. Before I could even pull off good, Niyah was ringing my phone again. I had been doing a pretty good job of ignoring her since yesterday, but now that the kids weren't around, I could finally talk about the shit with Judah in peace.

"Biiiiitch! Did you see that shit all over Facebook and the gram? I can't believe my hoe ass cousin! I been tryna call you since yesterday!" She squealed loudly as soon as I answered.

"Yeah, unfortunately I did and that's why I didn't answer. That's your cousin Kisha, the one you were tellin' me about?"

"Yeah, that's her ass but fuck her. What you tryna do friend? We can pull up on both they asses 'cause he got us fucked up!" I could hear her clapping as she spoke, and I laughed for what felt like the first time in 24 hours.

"Um, nah, boo. My pull up game is not strong," I admitted with a sigh. I was never the type to be in the middle of drama, and I wasn't about to start because Judah was on bull shit.

"Let me do the honors then 'cause that hoe need to catch somebody hands, feet, and mace!" She ranted. Niyah's ass had me dying laughing, but I knew she was dead ass serious. She was always ready to step. I guess we all had that one friend, and Niyah was mine.

"Calm down, killa. I can't be mad about him fuckin' around with that girl. I'm too old to be beefin' with anybody on the internet. Besides, I didn't have no business messin' with Judah's lil ass in the first place."

"Fuck all that. I'm tryna beat a bitch up. Yup! That hoe was outta order! She needs to be tryna get them kids back instead of showin' out, and Ju straight violated too. Girl, I'm so damn mad, I dropped my fuckin' cheeseburger!" She fumed, and I could hear her rustling around somewhere.

"Niyah, where the hell you at cursin' all loud and shit?"

"Oh girl, my mama made me come to some church picnic with her to volunteer, but I ain't helping them do shit but get rid of some of this food. It's all hot and shit- hold on, Nivea. Vickie, get yo' damn kids from over here, shit! Next time I'ma just keep goin' and knock one of they bad asses down!"

"Niyah, you cannot be up there talking like that around them church folks," I reprimanded, knowing damn well it was going in one ear and out the other.

"Please, ain't shit Godly 'bout half these people. Vickie ass got 3 kids by 3 different members of the church and ain't been married once. Girl, shut up! We all know yo' kids belong to all the deacons, and that shit nasty 'cause they old enough to be yo' daddy."

I laughed so hard at her going back and forth with the Vickie lady that I almost ran into another car on my way into the school's parking lot. I pulled into the first available spot I could find and got my stuff together while I listened to Niyah go off. I was happy I only had to meet with my math tutor today because it was my worst subject, so it would take my mind off all of the drama for an hour anyway.

"Niyah! Niyah! Stop arguing with that lady, girl. I gotta get in this library."

"This hoe far from a lady, but a'ight. I'ma get up with you later. Did you need a ride home?" She asked. I'd forgotten that I hadn't got a chance to tell her all about yesterday, starting with my car.

"Judah paid the repairs and had it dropped off yesterday before all this shit," I explained, waving a dismissive hand because he had lost every cool point he had gained by getting my car back with this fuck shit.

"Ohhhhh, hell naw, bitch! You gave him some didn't you!"

"I'ma tell you about it later, Niyah."

"That shit was good, huh? That young dick will turn ya out girl, and they just keep going and going-"

"I'm 'bouta hang up on you, bitch, but yessss, I'm still thinkin 'about it." I sighed and squeezed my eyes closed as my stomach tightened. No matter how mad I was at Judah, every time I thought about the orgasms he had given me, my body shook. Little piece of shit.

"Dammmmn, I need some details. I'm comin' over when you finish your session 'cause the day a nigga knocked the cobwebs off that pussy is a holiday!"

"Man, bye fool."

"Okay, see you later."

I spent the next 45 minutes ignoring calls and threatening texts from Judah. I didn't know if he had just noticed the post or if he had finally figured out what lie he wanted to spew, but he was a whole day late. If he really wanted me to even consider anything he had to say about the situation then he should have gotten to it right away. At this point, after reading all of the comments and shit, I didn't want to hear nothing from him.

As soon as the hour ended, I was out the door and ready to get home. The little bit of time I thought I would have to free my mind of my feelings towards Judah had been fucked up by him blowing up my phone. I wasn't trying to argue with him and if I talked to him right now, that's what was going to happen. No, the best thing for me to do right now would be to put his ass on the block list and move on with my life. That was easier said than done though because Judah was definitely hard to forget.

SAVAGE

I was going to kill Kisha when I caught up to her. Not only had she took the dick, and stopped me from going to Jay's mama crib, but she posted some bullshit ass picture on Facebook that had Nivea mad at me. I had tried calling her, but she either blocked me or just wasn't answering my shit. I didn't have time to be kissing Nivea's ass right now, especially about some goofy ass shit like this. If she didn't want to hear my side of the story, I wasn't about to beg her. Besides, I needed to get my mind right, so I could take care of this business with Jay.

I sat outside his mama house in a beater with my seat reclined all the way back and my gun out on my lap. My eyes were zeroed in on the front door waiting on any type of movement coming or going. I was hoping he would come soon though, so I ain't have to be out there all night. As much as I wanted to say fuck Nivea, the first thing I was going to do after I murked this nigga was pop up at her crib. Yeah, I was still pissed about her baby daddy, and she was acting crazy because of this shit with Kisha, but I wasn't gon' be able to just leave her alone. I told her she was mine and wasn't shit about to fuck that up. I let out a deep sigh because she was on my mind heavy after I'd just told myself that she wasn't going to be.

"Fuck is wrong with you, man? You over there huffin' and puffin' like a female," Pree observed from the side of me.

"Nigga, I just blew some air out. How the fuck I sound like a woman 'cause of that?" I sucked my teeth, mad that this nigga could already tell something was bothering me. That was exactly the problem with women. As soon as you let one in, you start doing little shit that let's muthafuckas know when y'all having issues.

"Cause nigga, that's the *I fucked up* face you wearing right now, and I know it ain't got shit to do with Jay. I done had it before," he said with a shrug that had me looking at him curiously. Pree didn't come off like the type that had issues with women. He was always on some old player shit. He never pressed no female that I ever saw. It wasn't like he had a bunch of different women around all the time, but I knew he was getting play from somebody.

"What you done had before, with yo old ass, Pree?"

"The shit face from fuckin' up with the woman I loved," He told me, and I choked on the blunt I was smoking.

"Love? Nah, bruh. I don't love these sneaky ass broads out here," I denied with a shake of my head. There was no way I loved Nivea this soon in the game. Hell nah. I'd just hit the pussy the other day and already I'd fucked somebody else and messed up whatever it was we were doing.

"I ain't say broads, nigga. I said a woman. It's a difference and you know it. A woman is somebody you trust, somebody you wanna make sure they're good, but you know she'll be good either way. You ain't supposed to fuck up with them types, they're rare." He took the blunt from my outstretched hand and puffed on it, holding in the smoke. He had just perfectly described Nivea. Could I really love her already? I wasn't experienced with love. I'd never met anybody that had made me feel any of the shit I felt with her, but did that mean I loved her?

"Stop lookin' stuck, lil nigga." He coughed. "Yo' ass in love. I'm just tryna hip you 'cause nobody ever put me on. Niggas was out here letting me run wild and telling me only weak niggas fell in love and gave up the life. Man, I fucked up with my one tryna play games and still be the man to a bunch of niggas that ain't even around no more. Got kids and every-thing, but she only let me be there financially 'cause she was worried about them getting hurt from being around me." He looked off out the window and even in the darkness I knew he was filled with regret. I was stuck. In five minutes Pree had admitted his ties to the streets and the fact that he had some kids out here. This nigga was trying to pour his heart out and shit right before I killed somebody.

"Fuck is you on, man? You talkin' 'bout me sounding like a woman and you out here on your Oprah shit."

"I ain't on shit. I'm spittin' real life facts to you. I'm tryna be the voice of reason for you that my niggas weren't for me," he said cooly, taking a sip of the drink he had.

"I'm good, old man. Put that bottle down. That damn henny got you in yo' chest for real."

"You might be right," he mumbled, squinting at what was left in his bottle. "Yeah, I'm fucked up, but remember what I said; they're rare. Don't fuck up like me, a'ight? After we take care of this, go get yo' girl."

"I got you, big dog," was all I said, bringing my attention back to the porch. I would definitely take the advice he'd given, but I ain't need my mind on that soft shit right now.

I sat up a little higher in my seat when I saw a hooded figure come through the backyard and walk up the stairs to the front door. I didn't even need to see his face to know it was Jay. He was the same height and build, and that walk was unmistakable. I tapped Pree on the arm and nudged my chin towards the porch. He followed my line of vision and nodded that he understood as I wrapped my hand around my gun. The rush I was feeling right then made it hard to wait on his mama to let him in, but I managed to stay still until he was inside.

I pulled the scarf that I had on up around my nose and mouth, so that I couldn't be identified, but there wasn't gon' be any witnesses. Closing the door quietly, I started towards the house, not even waiting around for Pree to actually get out the car. It wasn't like I needed him anyway, and he was drunk as hell. As I made my way into the yard, I could hear them going back and forth inside making it even harder for them to hear me walking up their raggedy ass steps.

"Jahque, stop comin' up in here all damn times of the night! Ain't nobody tryna get out the bed just to let yo' ass in!" His mama yelled loudly.

"If you gave me a key, I wouldn't have to knock! I'm out here running for my life and you worried 'bout me waking you up to get the door! Fuck is wrong with you?" I smiled inwardly at the fact that this nigga was openly admitting his fear.

I chose that moment to shoot the door knob. Jay immediately ran, and I sent a bullet through the back of his knee, dropping him. His mama stood there screaming 'til I pointed my gun in her face. "Shut up bitch!" She muffled her own sobs by throwing her hands over her mouth. I made my way further into the house to where Jay was trying to struggle away. "Nigga, where the fuck you think you goin'?" I laughed and sent a kick to his ribcage. "Yo' mama already mad about getting outta bed, now you 'bouta die and fuck up her floors."

"Fuck you, Savage!" He grimaced, turning over onto his back. I kicked his little bitch ass again, gaining a scream out of him.

"You think I give a fuck 'bout you sayin' my name, pussy?" I laughed again and snatched the scarf I was wearing off my face. "All you just did was make the decision to kill this bitch for me." His eyes widened as I aimed and shot his mama right between the eyes.

"Damn ,man! My fuckin' mama tho?" The hurt look on his face ended up covered by my boot. His nose instantly squirted more blood out, and he covered it with one hand. I crouched down beside him, ready to get this shit over with.

"You killed yo' mama, my nigga. Shit, at least you won't be going to hell alone. She was a bitch anyway." I shrugged, emptying my clip in his face. Blood and brain matter splattered all over my face and I used my scarf to wipe it off. "Hoe ass nigga."

"Ju, let's get the fuck outta here, man." Pree's voice broke through the silence that had now filled the room. He tapped my shoulder like I ain't hear him and I stood. "Just couldn't wait for me, huh?"

"Nah, I had it under control." I shrugged, side stepping Jay's body as Pree fell in step beside me.

"And the bitch?" He pointed at Jay's mama crumpled up by the door.

"He did that," was all I said, exiting like I hadn't just killed them both. Pree let out a whistle and mumbled something under his breath, but I couldn't make it out. Honestly, I didn't even care because I'd finally handled the business for Troy. Now all I had to do was get my girl back.

After I'd cleaned up, put away my guns and disposed of the car, I made my way to Nivea's crib unsure of what exactly I was going to say. I knew she was mad and shit, and probably had expected an explanation for that Facebook shit, but even if I told her, she wouldn't believe me. How fucking crazy would it sound if I told her that Kisha's dumb ass drugged me, especially since I pop pills on the regular. I still didn't even believe that shit. Probably the only way she would even listen was if I had some proof. On a whim, I shot Kisha a text hoping that her obsession with me would make her answer. I was hoping that as soon as she saw that it wasn't a threat, she would answer my shit honestly, but I was still gone kill her ass.

Me: Kisha, what the fuck u give me, man? That shit done had me sick since yesterday.

I was anxious as fuck waiting on her to reply. This was going to at least get Nivea to hear me out instead of immediately dismissing me. It finally showed that she had read it, but I knew she was going to take a minute to decide whether or not she should admit to actually putting some shit in my food.

Thatcraxybitch: Ju, all I gave you was melatonin. It shouldn't have made you sick.

I knew her ass was lying, but it would still show that she had admitted to giving me something. I googled that shit and saw that it was something to help people sleep. It was a big chance that Nivea was still gone send my ass home even if she let me show her the text. Little did she know, I wasn't letting her go that easy. I felt my phone vibrating and knew that it was another text from Kisha, but I'd gotten what I needed from her for now. I ended up having to park up the street from her apartment, but I wasn't tripping about the short walk. It gave me more time to figure out what I was going to say when she answered the door.

By the time I'd made it in front of her building, I had it worked out in my head how this shit was going to go, and it was definitely ending with me spending the night. Well, that was the thought until I saw her sitting out front with her bitch ass baby daddy.

NIVEA

*T*he day had turned out not to be so bad after all. Well, after Niyah came over with some patron and made daiquiris. We sat out on my stoop listening to Trey Songz station on Pandora while I filled her in on the most recent things that had happened between me and Judah. After I told her about the way he'd snatched my soul and then had breakfast and my car waiting on me the next morning, she was all team Judah again.

"Girl, fuck Judah," I said way louder than I'd intended to. Her ass had me out here feeling myself a little too hard with these drinks.

"Nah, see these hoes be out here setting niggas up. Ain't no way he went through all that trouble the morning he left just to turn around and let that bum bitch Kish post them pics." she told me matter of factly.

"That's yo' whole damn cousin, Niyah."

"So, she still a bum ass hoe, cousin or not." She shrugged.

"Bitch, you so damn wishy washy," I cracked. "Just this morning you was gon' beat a bitch up and now you actin' like you Judah's defense attorney." I looked at her sideways as she gulped down the last of her drink and frowned from the brain freeze.

"I'm still ready to beat that hoe Kisha's ass, but as far as Ju, I think he might have been tricked by that sneaky bitch. I been lookin' at the picture, and he def look sleep." She started to pull her phone out to show me, but I'd seen the picture enough. I wasn't trying to see it again, or study it to see if Judah looked sleep like she claimed.

"Nope, I ain't even tryna see that shit." I turned away, waving her off. Besides, seeing that hoe all over him was bad enough. But the fact that she had one of those perfect Instagram bodies made it even more difficult to see. It brought out insecurities I had about my pudgy belly, my stretch marks, and how my breasts and ass had a slight sag to them. Things that I was sure nobody Judah had ever fucked had going on besides me. He had all types of video vixen, buffy the body built bitches at his disposal, and it just felt like maybe he was settling with me. I'm sure if I told Niyah about my feelings, she would curse me out. So, I didn't have no intentions on telling her mean ass.

"Well, I'm rootin' for him, friend. Y'all cute together," she said, pouring herself some more drink into her glass.

"Ma! Ma! QJ tryna hog the tv, and Kymia lettin' him!"

"No! It's my turn, Nana!"

I turned around to see QJ and Quiana standing in the door pushing each other. Niyah laughed on the side of me as I took my time standing up. I wasn't drunk, but I was feeling that damn Patron.

"Shut up, Niyah." I threw over my shoulder. "Let me go get them situated. I'll be back."

"Okay."

"Y'all stop acting crazy. It's time for y'all to go to bed anyway," I said, separating them by picking up QJ. For them to be so close, they were always fighting. Of course, they both started huffing and puffing about having to go to bed.

"But ma, it's the summer time. Why can't we stay up late?" Quiana whined.

"Should have thought about that before y'all started fighting. It's obvious y'all sleepy. Come on." I ignored the way her eyebrows drew together as she pouted and started up the stairs with a fairly content QJ still in my arms.

"But maaaaa!"

"Quiana, I know you better bring yo' ass upstairs." I gave her the *I'm gone beat your ass* face and she blew out a deep breath before passing me and stomping up the steps. "Stop stompin'!" I followed her up to our apartment and headed straight to the bathroom to run them some water for a bath.

Thirty minutes later, they were all bathed and in bed after a few struggles besides Kymia, who was in the living room watching tv. As long as she left me alone, I was gonna leave her alone. The sky was starting to get darker, letting me know that it wouldn't be too much longer that we would be outside. I wasn't about to play with these little niggas out here ready to shoot first and ask questions later. By the time I got downstairs, Niyah was still in the same spot except now she was joined by some little dread head. I can admit that he was cute even though I could never get with the whole dreads thing. Something about a man with hair hanging all in his face didn't do it for me.

"See, this my friend right here!" She said loudly as soon as she saw me. I gave a sheepish smile and waved politely, but I was not tryna be in their conversation.

"Wassup," he mumbled, giving me a head nod.

"Now you can get yo' guy out the car, and we can turn this into a party!" Niyah cheesed, nudging me as I sat down. I shook my head fast because I was already in some shit with one nigga. I didn't need to add another one to the mix.

"Riiiight," he dragged, rubbing a hand across his beard. "Let me go get him." He took off before I could even fix my lips to object, and I turned and gave Niyah the death stare.

"Whaaaaat? You said you wanted to take yo' mind off Ju." She shrugged like she ain't hear how dumb she sounded.

"Bitch, I'ma slap yo drunk ass. I don't need to find no new nigga! Did you forget about Quad?" I asked. She rolled her eyes at that and waved me off.

"Girl, Quad ass don't count," she snickered. Since I didn't really have a valid comeback for that, I chose to remain silent. No, in the grand scheme of things Quad didn't really count considering that he still had seven years left on his sentence, but he was still someone...sort of. "Exactly bitch, don't say nothin' 'cause you already know!"

"Nivea?"

That fucking voice made me cringe hard as hell. Who would have known that when dude said he had a friend, it was none other than Ky's clown ass. I released a deep sigh because I wasn't trying to be bothered with him. I hadn't even seen him since that night at the club.

"Oh, hell naw! This yo' friend?" Niyah asked, frowning. "Nope, nope, nope! I'm good. If you hang with dead beats, then you are a dead beat."

"Dead beat what? My nigga takes care of his son," the dude said stupidly, and I just shook my head. I don't even know why it surprised me that this dumb ass nigga didn't know about Kymia. If Ky would deny her to me of course he would deny her to the world.

"You sound dumb as fuck! This boy got a whole teenager with her." Niyah pointed my way while me and Ky had a stare down.

"Mannn, I ain't got no baby by this broad, on foe and 'em. You out here fuckin' rappers and shit. Go pin yo' baby on one of them niggas. I outta beat yo' ass for that shit at the club," Ky said, flexing in front of his friend.

"Nigga, I wish you would!" Niyah cut in, stopping her conversation briefly.

"What the fuck you gon' do?" Ky grilled her hard. It was always the niggas that were scared to fight another man that stayed getting buck with women. Ky didn't even raise his voice at Judah, but since it was just me and Niyah, he felt comfortable making threats.

"I thought I told you to stay away from her?"

*M*y eyes bucked at Judah approaching looking just as good as he had yesterday. I had to remind myself that I was mad at his little lying ass. Ky must have been feeling himself 'cause his friend was there. Instead of moving the fuck around, he turned to Judah like he was tough.

"And like I told you last time, mind yo' fuckin business, nigga. I got a burner today too. It ain't shit to bust it." He puffed out his chest and said, gaining a fake laugh from Judah and a look of pity from me and Niyah. We had seen what happened at the club and knew that even without a gun, Judah could beat his ass. His friend who had been silent this whole time started shaking his head.

"Man, what the fuck you on, my nigga? I fucks with Ju."

Ky looked around obviously feeling outnumbered since his friend was scared and sucked his teeth.

"Don't get quiet now, bitch boy!" Niyah's ratchet ass said with a grin. I guess he wanted to save face 'cause he still didn't leave, but by now, it was too late. Judah seemed like he grew wings and was in front of him like he flew.

"Don't no nigga put fear in my heart, especially not this lil nigga!" And just like that, he was on the ground. Judah had hit him so hard that as soon as he landed, he was snoring. As bad as I wanted to stay mad at him, I couldn't help being turned on.

"Get this nigga from in front of here!" Judah barked at Ky's friend, who immediately threw his hands up in defense. Without even taking a second glance, Judah turned to me with his face contorted. "Bring yo' ass here, Nivea!" He pointed directly in front of him like I was his child.

I shook my head *no* defiantly. There was no way I was going anywhere near him right now. If he thought he could just come over here demanding shit, he had another thing coming. I didn't care how wet he was making me by bossing up the way he was. It still didn't change the fact that he left me to go be with his girlfriend that I knew nothing about.

"No! You can't be coming over here yelling at me and shit after yesterday. You better take yo' ass back to yo' girlfriend," I scoffed childishly. Yeah, I know I was acting my shoe size, but he had to know that it wasn't going to be that easy.

"That bitch ain't my girl, man. I could have told you that if you ain't block me." He gave me a pointed look, and Niyah coughed to cover up her saying, "Good point". I was starting to get so used to rolling my eyes at her that I didn't even realize I'd done it before bringing my attention back to Judah.

"Really? Cause that picture of her half-naked in yo' lap says otherwise. Why even waste my time, Judah? You know what I'm about. All I do is take care of my kids and work! I don't have time to be worrying about you and some secret ass girlfriend!"

"Oh, like yo' secret baby daddy? Or he don't count 'cause he in jail?" He asked, cocking his head to the side and pinning me with a stare. I looked away, unable to meet his eyes.

"You never asked," I replied weakly.

"Exactly! You ain't ask either! But if you woulda, then I could have told you that I don't. Kisha just a broad I used to fuck around with. There was never no title there! You just let a nigga in. We ain't get a chance to talk about all that irrelevant ass shit."

"Yeah and you fucked up that quick! I might kinda still be with Quad, but ain't shit physical there! Ain't been in three years! Can you tell me the same? Can you say you ain't fuck her yesterday?" I didn't really want to know the answer to that. It would make it that much harder to let him go, even though I already suspected that he did. I was putting up a hard front like I could handle it if he said that he'd left my bed to go fuck that girl. But in reality, it was going to hurt to be disappointed yet again.

"I ain't gone lie, I let shorty in on some cool shit. I was still feeling some type of way about you and yo' bd. We ate and shit, a nigga fell asleep." He shrugged. "When I woke up, shorty was sittin' on me snappin' pictures. I put her ass out so fast, I ain't even realize she was doing that shit off my phone until niggas started commenting and shit. By that time, I knew you had saw it, but yo' ass blocked me without giving me a chance to explain." I had to admit that his story seemed possible, but he had me fucked up if he thought I was going to believe that bullshit. I was a grown ass woman who had dated more than a few liars, so I wasn't about to just believe whatever he told me. There was probably some truth to what he was saying but him just waking up to her in his lap wasn't it.

"So, you want me to believe that you fell asleep, Judah? And then you woke up with her damn near naked in yo' lap and didn't fuck?"

"Yes! I need you to believe me 'cause I ain't hit that crazy ass bitch, a'ight!" He said, towering over me. "Look, we both fucked up. Let's just put this shit behind us and start over." His voice had gotten considerably lower and he put his fore- head against mine as he tried to reason with me. It seemed so natural the way I fit into his arms, and he pulled me close, but it could have just been the lack of affection I'd been missing since Quad had been gone.

"I don't know, Judah." I closed my eyes as I shook my head. This wasn't just some regular ass hood gossip. It was all over social media. He had even admitted to being associated with the girl. I wasn't trying to get caught up in some TMZ ass love triangle with a nigga that was years younger than me. There were so many ways that this could go wrong.

"What don't you know, shorty? You know I'm feelin you hard as fuck, and you know I hit that pussy right. That's all we need to worry 'bout right now." The ache I felt between my legs when he said that had my knees weak. I didn't want to be one of them weak ass females that melted every time a nigga with good dick said some sweet shit to me, but Judah was already taking over more than just my body. His little ass was taking over my heart.

"Damn." I'd forgotten all about Niyah's nosy ass standing there until she said that and started slow clapping like we were at the movies and shit. "You better say that shit, Ju!"

I couldn't help but to laugh at her extra ass as she stood there dabbing at her eyes. I hadn't even said okay or nothing, and she already knew I was about to give in. "Oh my God, Niyah." I covered my face with my hands.

"What? I told you I was team Ju, bitch," she said, sticking out her tongue at me. "So, y'all 'bouta take this upstairs and make it official or nah?"

"Bye, Niyah!"

"I'm going, I'm going," she huffed, gathering up her things and waving good bye over her head. "Make sure you fuck the doubt out her, Ju!"

"See, yo' friend already know what it is," Judah said, giving me that sexy grin of his. "Come let me holla at you upstairs."

I didn't fight him as he wrapped my hand in his and led me into the hallway. "My kids up there," I whispered like they could hear us from all the way in our apartment.

"I'ma make sure you keep it down," he told me, leading me to the door. I stepped in first to see if Kymia was still up, but surprisingly, she wasn't in the living room anymore and the tv was off. Putting a finger to my lips, I ushered Judah inside, and tried to get him into my bedroom without making any noise. My kids could hear the smallest thing and would know I was up, and I wasn't trying to take no chances.

"Ma?" Kymia's voice filled the small hallway just as I shoved Judah inside my room.

"Huh?" I wasn't sure if it was just me or not, but my voice was shaky as hell. It was crazy how worried I was about having a man in my house where I paid bills, but like I said, I didn't bring a lot of men around my kids.

"Nothing, I was just makin' sure you came in ok. You not allowed to stay out so late." She twisted her lips and raised her brows at me.

"Uh, ok, mama," I replied smartly. "Now take yo' lil ass to bed." It was rare for Kymia to play or joke around, but when she did, I tried to hold on to those moments because it was no telling when they would happen again. She rolled her eyes playfully and I waited while she shut the door back before going into my room, making sure to lock the knob behind me.

"I guess she told yo' ass," Judah joked as soon I was safely inside. He was sitting on the bed looking comfortable like everything was cool.

"I'm not 'bouta play with you, Judah. You still on punishment, my nigga."

"Listen at you talkin' 'bout *my nigga* like you with the shits," he teased, flashing that perfect smile and stood up from his spot on the bed.

"I'm serious. We still need to talk about whatever this is." I pointed between the two of us. "You still got a girlfriend, and my baby daddy is still in the picture. Don't you think that's important?"

He ran a hand down his handsome face and let out a long sigh. "Nah, we don't gotta talk about shit 'cause you already know what this is."

"That sounds like bullshit! *I know what this is.*" I scoffed mocking his voice. "I don't know shit but that you left me and never answered your phone, but your girlfriend did, then I woke up to all types of pictures of you and her."

"Fuck that bitch. I told you what happened. Fuck I need to lie for?" He held his arms open with hunched shoulders.

"Shit, I don't know. It's so many reasons why niggas lie these days! Is this a joke to you? Is it some kind of test to see if you can get an older woman? Like, what do you want with me, Judah, when you have girls like Kisha chasing behind you? I'm grown as hell, got 3 kids, 2 baby daddies, bills, a belly, stretch marks and bad ass credit! I don't need the added stress from you!" I hissed loudly. Well, as loud as I could without waking up my damn kids. It wasn't that I was trying to release all of my insecurities to him at one time, but he needed to know that I had enough problems without adding a dick slinging ass young nigga to the equation. I could tell that by the time I was done, he would better understand what he was getting himself into, but it's not like that ever mattered to niggas anyway.

"You done?" He questioned, crossing his arms over his chest and looking at me unbothered. That only brought my level of irritation up more.

"No!"

"Well say what you tryna say, so I can gon' head and shoot that shit down." His voice was nonchalant like he hadn't heard a damn thing I'd said, or he just didn't give a fuck. Either way, he couldn't change the way I felt about it.

"Did you hear what I said? I don't need you wasting my time." I fought to keep from crying and wondered when I had become so damn emotional about Judah.

"Nivea," he said slowly, and a bitch felt real life chills. As he spoke, he made his way across the room, stopping right in front of me. "I told you this shit is new to me, but everything about you, even the shit you just named, is something to admire."

"Phstt." How the fuck was any of that shit something to be admired? I wasn't ashamed of my situation, but I wasn't proud of it either. I just did what I needed to do every day to get by. That was just what I was taught though.

"Shorty, you think I see that shit when I look at you? The only thing that be on my mind when I'm around you is *damn she's smart, she's beautiful, she's strong*. That's way sexier than a big booty slide. Shit, I don't know about these other niggas, but I can appreciate a strong black woman. I'm not tryna play with you. I'm serious when I say I wanna see where this shit goin'." I let him pull me against his body without fighting, but I remained limp in his arms. He buried his face in my neck like always and inhaled. And just like that, I already knew that he had got me. Damn, I hope I don't regret this!

SAVAGE

$\mathcal{H}$ ours later after we'd talked until Nivea fell asleep, I sat awake thinking about the things she'd said. I didn't want to be the cause of more pain for her, and I damn sure didn't want to feed her insecurities. What really happened with Kisha couldn't ever get out or would ruin the little bit of trust she had in me? I wasn't too worried about that happening though because as soon as I found that bitch, she was dying right along with Keys. I looked over at her sleeping with her mouth wide open and shook my head. Shorty had me wide open and ain't even know. What was crazier was the fact that she hadn't even tried. It was going to be hard to convince her that I was for real about what I was feeling for her.

I grabbed my phone off of her nightstand and deleted the posts that Kisha had put on my instagram and then did the same for my Facebook since I hadn't gotten a chance to earlier. That bitch had gotten a ton of likes and comments talking about how we were the next Durk and India, and some other stupid shit. I could have just written back on that shit, and blasted Kisha for flodging so hard, but I thought of a much more direct approach. Grabbing Nivea's phone, I looked for the softest shit I could find, which was pretty much everything on there. It was full of old 90s cuts that my OG used to listen to when I was little. I looked over at shorty and laughed. She was a straight up lame, but I was feeling that.

Out of all the tracks she had, Nivea's *25 Reasons* stood out. Probably because they had the same name. I remember one of the females I fucked with before had played it for me, but it didn't really mean shit at the time. Now it was meaningful because I fucked with Nivea on a deeper level than any girl I'd been with. I played the track a few times as I got my words together before finding the instrumentals on YouTube. Once I had it down, I selected the live feature on my Facebook. Almost immediately people joined. It was bitches asking to join me and putting heart eyes on my shit while niggas tried to act like we were cool, but I wasn't on shit besides getting my point across.

"Aye, I'm 'bouta spit somethin' for my shorty right quick. That shit that Kish put up earlier got her feeling some type of way, so I'ma clear this up so it ain't no confusion. Nivea is my present and future and this the first step in showing her that. Call this the Nivea challenge." I started the instrumentals and made sure that Nivea was visible in the camera before flowing.

Bae, why you actin' like that, you must don't know this but shorty you bad
Got me thinkin' bout settling down and getting things I never had
You think that I look at you different cuz you a lil older, but that shit don't matter to me
Them stretch marks ain't shit, and that lil belly
Don't matter to a muhfuckin' G

When I'm in the streets you think I be cheatin', I don't understand
it I swear you be tweakin'
Let's make this official, and stop all this beefin'
I wanna be with you and that ain't no secret
You got that good, good hold down two jobs
And on top of that bae you a cutie
Why would I ever jeopardize all of that for a thot bitch or a groupie
When I'm in the streets, I stay on them bands
And fuckin' with hoes ain't in the plan
I gotta real one in you shorty
So why would I give them a chance
You gotta understand that before I met you I was out here runnin'
wild
But that ain't the same me, ma you changed me
So let's gon' head settle down
Bitches be hatin' and makin' shit up they only concerned with
breakin' us up
I'm done with that life, I gave that shit up so here go my jersey
hang that shit up

By the time I finished, I had five hundred viewers and more than a thousand comments. There were a few haters, but it was mostly all love. The sound of her door creaking open took my attention away from my phone to see her little man peeking in. I looked back at Nivea not really sure of what to do since she really ain't want me to meet them yet, but she was still knocked out. Kids were weird as fuck 'cause apparently I wasn't loud enough to wake up Nivea, but his little ass heard me from a whole 'nother room. He stood there in the doorway for a second probably trying to figure out who the fuck I was before he padded over to where I was sitting on the edge of the bed.

"Who is you?" He questioned, tilting his head.

"Wassup man, I'm Ju. What's yo' name?" I didn't really

know what to say. I was still shocked that he ain't spazz out as soon as he saw me.

"I'm Quad, but everybody calls me Qj," he mumbled and looked pass me to where Nivea lay snoring.

"Q jizzy." I laughed and reached out for a dap. "It's nice to meet you, homie." He bumped his small fist with mine and giggled at my nickname. I could tell already that we were gonna be tight. At least I had one of her shorties rocking with me. "You tryna sleep with yo' mama tonight?"

"Yeah, Quiana was kickin me." He nodded while talking like just telling me wasn't good enough. "My mama never kicks."

"Well good luck, my nigga. She might not kick you, but she damn sho' ain't gon' let you sleep wit' how loud she snoring," I joked, and he laughed like he understood exactly what I was talking about. "You know her ass loud, huh?"

"Yeah, she's pretty loud." He shrugged with his grown ass. I could already tell me and him would get along; he was a smart little dude. He climbed up next to me on the bed and curled right up like he knew me. Yeah, he was gon' be my lil homie. "You stayin'?"

I shot a glance back at Nivea and scratched my neck. I wasn't sure if she was gon' be cool with me chilling with her son, but if we was gon' be together then I planned on being around him a whole lot. "Yeah, I'ma be here, Q jizzy."

"Okay, but my name is Quuuaaad." I could see him bucking his eyes at me while he said it like I was slow or something, and I chuckled.

"A'ight, Quuuuaaad, gone head and go to sleep," I told him, lying back with my arm tucked under my head. I was tired as fuck, but little dude kept me up for another hour asking me questions and shit until he couldn't fight his sleep anymore and finally closed his eyes, and I was right behind him.

NIVEA

J woke up to all types of screaming and tried to cover my head with the pillow. "Omg y'all! It's too early to be so loud!" I'd forgotten all about Judah being here last night and how I had fallen asleep on him. Opening my eyes, I realized that he was the reason for all the yelling I heard coming from the girls.

"I know you not sleep, Judah. You might as well get up and meet them 'cause they're not 'bouta stop." I laughed. His lips curved up into a slick grin, but he kept his eyes closed.

"A nigga sleep, man."

I went to push his ass out the bed, but Quad's little body lay between us. I didn't even know he had wiggled his way into my bed. Usually he would be all over me, but he was curled up next to Judah like they were best friends.

"When the hell he get in here?" I mused aloud. Judah peeked open one eye and looked at Quad laying beside him.

"Oh, Q jizzy came in here last night after you fell asleep. Sat up for like an hour talking and shit. Are kids always like that?" He questioned with an amused face. That was surprising. Quad wasn't mean or nothing, but he didn't automatically talk to strangers. The fact that he saw Judah in my bed and didn't have a fit was throwing me, but I played it off well.

"Q jizzy??" I gave him a funny look.

"Yeah, he cool. Let him rock his nickname."

"A'ight, well Q jizzy and almost every other kid in the world talks a lot. Your whole ear can fall off and they'd probably still be talking." The look on his face had me dying laughing on the inside. He must didn't know kids ask more questions than a little bit, but he would definitely be finding out.

We both still had yet to acknowledge the girls in the room who were both still dancing, waiting on Judah to get up. Kymia was on the phone with her best friend and Quiana was trying to show him dances even though he hadn't even lifted his head up.

"Come on and talk to these two before their heads explode from excitement."

"A'ight. Aye, what's up, y'all?" He said, sitting up on his elbows. They both froze in place, shocked that the infamous Ju Savage was in their house speaking to them. Kymia was the first to speak.

"Oh my God! Amiyah, Ju Savage spoke to me!" She screamed, running out of the room. Quaina waited until she had cleared the hall before turning back to us with her hand on her hip.

"Did you see me dancing?" She wanted to know.

"Uhhh, yeah," he lied quickly, making her roll her eyes.

"So, can I be in the next video then?" Judah fell out laughing while she stood in the same spot waiting on his reply with a hand on her hip. When he realized she was serious, he stopped laughing and looked at me.

"I ain't got nothin' to do with that." I shrugged with a chuckle.

"You got that lil miss…"

"Quiana," she told him firmly, coming over and shaking his hand to seal the deal.

"Lil Miss Quiana, okay."

"I'm for real too. Don't be tryna back out. I need my coins." She tilted her head and said before leaving my room.

"What the fuck was that?" Judah asked, looking amazed and confused at the same time.

"That was just a 10-year old in 2018," I joked even though it was true. Kids these days said and did some crazy stuff, and I had been more than a little surprised by some of the shit that came out Quiana's mouth sometimes. He shook his head probably thinking how crazy that conversation just was, but he didn't look irritated, which was a plus. I had actually not planned on him meeting the kids for awhile. At least until I knew for sure that he wasn't on bullshit with me. I know that children often overwhelmed niggas and since he was so young and didn't have any kids, I didn't want him to feel pressured into anything.

"Wowwww." He dragged and tried to sit all the way up, but Quad started moving, so he froze up.

"It's cool. He's probably 'bouta wake up anyway. All of them get up early as hell." I reassured and started to get up myself. Judah followed suit and Quad's eyes popped open. "See?"

"Yeah." He laughed, giving QJ, who was already standing up on my bed, a pound. "What's up, Q jizzy?"

"Sup, Ju!" He said, giggling at his nickname.

"You wanna go grab some food?" Judah paused his playing with QJ and looked at me expectantly.

"Yeah, I could eat. You hungry, Quad?"

"Yes! And I'm Q jizzy now, ma." He had the nerve to say.

"Boy, I am not callin' yo' lil ass Q jizzy. I'ma leave that to Judah." He just laughed at me and continued to jump up and down. Little bad ass. "Let me go get my hygiene straight," I told Judah, grabbing my phone from the nightstand.

The girls had disappeared into another part of the house, so I could brush my teeth. I had barely got the toothpaste on when my phone started buzzing with a call from Niyah.

"Hey girl." I gushed.

"Biiiiiiitch! Did you see the video? That shit 'bouta be viral in a minute!"

"What video?" I asked around my toothbrush, confused.

"Judah went live last night and started a Nivea challenge! Girl, he was all on that shit braggin' about you with you sleep in the background. I don't know how yo' ass ain't hear him." I spit out the toothpaste I had in my mouth and stood there dumbfounded.

"What you mean a challenge, and I was sleep, bitch? I'ma beat Judah's ass." I gasped in horror and covered my face with my hands.

"It's cute, Nivea, relax. He just wanted the world to know that he's with you and not Kisha. It's like how Chance the rapper started the So Gone challenge." She told me like that made it any better. "Just go check it out before you have a panic attack over nothing; it's on Ju's page." The silence on the line let me know that she had hung up.

I wasted no time going straight to Judah's Facebook and it happened to be the last thing he had posted. I watched as he talked for a second, flashing the camera on me before going into his rap. Tears welled up in my eyes at some of the things he was saying about me. While I wasn't happy about him putting me online while I was sleep, it was still extremely sweet and his way of showing me that I was who he wanted.

I hurried to finish brushing my teeth and left the bathroom to go find him. All of the noise was coming from the living room, so I looked there first. Quad was sitting on the couch watching cartoons and Quiana was sitting next to him with her tablet in her lap. "Where did Judah go?" I questioned.

"He got a call and said he had to go." She shrugged. "But did you see the video he made? I'm glad he didn't show you slobbing. That woulda been embarrassing," she told me with a snicker. I was a little salty that Judah hadn't told me he was leaving, but if it was an emergency, I understood. He did have a friend in the hospital.

"Oh okay, welllll, what do you think about me and Judah being friends?" I took the opportunity to ask. She squinted up at me as she thought for a minute before saying.

"You don't gotta say friends, ma," she rolled her eyes. "He likes you. I guess I'm cool with it. Does that mean you not with my daddy no more?"

"Yeah, are you leavin' daddy for Ju?" Kymia came into the room, plopping down on the couch next to her siblings.

"Nooo, I'm not leavin' Quad for Judah. But I do think that we shouldn't be together right now, and I do want to see how this goes with Judah," I explained slowly, trying to make sure that they understood.

"Well, I like Judah. It's okay if you don't wanna be with daddy. We can still see him tho, right?" Quiana mused, looking up at me indifferently and I instantly felt bad for not taking them to see their father these last few weeks.

"Yeah, now since we got the car back, we can start back going to see him, baby." I nodded.

"I'm cool with you being with Ju too, ma. It ain't like daddy act right anyways," Kymia added, and I wondered what she meant by that. Before I could ask though, my phone started ringing with a call from my mama.

"Ma, let me call you back," I rushed, thinking that she was calling me about Judah's video as I eyed Kymia, who was snuggled up with her brother.

"No, Nivea, its important! They found Brenda and Jay dead in her house!" She shouted in my ear.

"Wait, what!" I shrieked, gaining the attention of the kids. I had literally just been arguing with this lady yesterday, and now she was dead. How was I supposed to tell Quad that his mama and his brother were killed? I may not have liked Brenda most of the time and I for damn sure didn't like Jay, but I wouldn't wish death on nobody.

"They're dead, Nivea! Somebody came in her house and killed them last night. I bet you it had something to do with Jay's no good ass. That boy stays pissing somebody off." She tsked, and I could imagine her shaking her head.

"Ma, I'ma call you back," I sighed, falling back into the chair that was behind me.

"Okay baby, I'm praying for you and my grand babies. If you need me, just call." She told me. I don't even remember saying anything back before I just hung up. How was I going to explain this to the kids? And how could I just leave Quad alone with seven years left, and his only family dead. There was no way I would be able to leave him to face this alone. Could I?

"Kids, I gotta tell y'all something."

SAVAGE

I hated to dip out on Nivea and the kids, but Pree called me from the hospital to tell me that Troy had woken up. I had been in the middle of answering questions from Quiana and playing with Q jizzy, but I got out of there quick when I got that call. When I got to the hospital, my mama and little sister were there hugging all on Troy who was sitting up in bed. It felt good as fuck to see my homie's eyes finally open.

"Bring yo' ass over here, nigga," he croaked hoarsely and my OG slapped his ass in the head.

"Don't be cussin' boy," she snapped and then started straightening his covers before moving back so that I could take her place beside his bed.

"Dang ma, you can't be slappin' him up, and he just came out a coma," I teased, making my way over. "How you beat me up here anyway?" I dapped up Pree who was sitting in a chair near the bed.

"Pree called me." She shrugged. I looked between the two of them curiously but figured I would ask them about that shit later. They were getting way too cool for me.

"Man, what's up. I missed yo' nappy head ass," I said, giving Troy a manly hug, making sure to not hurt him. My mama hit me right in the back and hissed under her breath.

"Whateva nigga, you know it's gon' take more than a bullet to take Trigga out," he boasted with a wide grin. Janiah sucked her teeth at that and fell back into the other chair in the room.

"I'm already knowing. Hey, fat head." I finally spoke to my little sister, and she gave me a dry ass *hey* in return. Since there was such a huge age gap between us, I never really spent too much time with her, but I could already see what Nivea was talking about with these 2018 kids.

"You know I ate that for you too, right?" I brought my gaze back to Troy. His eyes brightened at my code for having killed Jay and he nodded and bumped my fist.

"Appreciate that, but did you save me some?"

I shook my head no regrettably. "Nah man, it was long overdue that I got that, so I ate the whole thing." Again, he nodded his understanding. I know my homie wanted a piece of the Jay pie, but I had to take his ass down. It was more than a matter of principal. However, it was still the matter of Keys bitch ass lurking around, and Kish. "I got something else you might like tho, I'ma hip you."

"Okay, enough of that fake ass code y'all got goin' on. Do you need somethin', Troy? I gotta go and grab something to eat," my OG fussed, causing us to chuckle. She swears she knoww some shit.

"Nah, Ms. Jackie, I'm good. I ain't been woke a full day and I'm already tired of this hospital food."

"I didn't say I was getting nothing from outta here. Hmph, they not 'bouta poison me," she quipped. "Now what you want before I change my mind?"

Troy leaned back and put a finger under his chin like he was in deep thought. "Can I get some Harold's?"

"Yep, that's right on the way. Come on, Niah." My sister looked up from her phone and followed my mama to the door.

"Make sure they add lemon pepper and mild sauce!" Troy yelled out.

"Boy, I got this. Pree, come walk a young lady to her car. Can't be too careful out here. Some lady and her son were killed in their home last night." She frowned at the thought.

"You got it, Jack," he said, standing to his feet and following her out the door.

I had been so busy being stuck on the fact that my mama knew about Jay and his mama that I didn't notice right away that Pree had called her Jack. I told Troy I'd be right back and headed down the stairs, hoping to catch Pree on his way back up. Lucky for me, I didn't have to because they were on the first floor standing at the entrance. As soon as I saw them having what looked like a heated discussion, I backed up, so they couldn't see me. Janiah wasn't around so I assumed she had sent her to the car, so they could talk in private.

"Jessiah, the only reason I agreed to you being around was to keep him out of trouble and now he upstairs talkin' about he was involved in that shit with Brenda!" My OG hissed angrily.

"And I been doin' a good fuckin' job keeping him out of trouble. His lil ass stay in the studio, and he on the verge of getting a deal. He felt like he needed to get at that nigga, and I allowed him to do that safely. Ain't no fuckin' way he gon' get caught," said Pree or as my mama called him, Jessiah. I stood there behind a damn plant trying to figure out what reason my mama would have for trying to assign his ass to baby sit me.

"Listen at you talkin' all street and shit. I guess underneath all this "new shit", it's still the same old Supreme huh? I told you I didn't want my son in the streets!"

"OUR son, Jack. He's our son and they're our fuckin' kids! Stop talkin' down on me a'ight, 'cause when I was out here, yo' ass was right out here with me!" He barked, pointing a finger at her. It took a lot to shock my ass these days, but to find out that me and my sister were the kids he was talking about last night had my mouth falling open.

"You better watch yo' tone with me, Jessiah! Yes! I was out there with you until I found out I was going to be a parent. I grew up like I was supposed to but you-"

"Jackie, what you want from me, huh?" He cut her off. "I been grown. It was my grown ass that bought you that fuckin' bakery, it's my grown ass that's taking care of OUR kids even though you weren't tryna let me see them, and when you want some dick, it's my grown ass comin' over to my house to give you this pipe! Stop tryna play me like a chump, Jackie."

I couldn't take no more. I had to let my presence be known before they said some more shit I didn't want to hear. I stepped around the plant, gaining the attention of my mama who gasped, making Pree turn my way. "So, this my fuckin' father?" I questioned, walking up on them both. Pree stepped up in front of my mama like I would hurt her or some shit, making me angrier than I was.

"Watch yo' mouth talkin' to yo' mama nigga!" He growled, staring me down.

"Fuck out my face, my nigga!" I wasn't trying to hear shit he had to say. His ass had been MIA my whole life and thought just because he had popped up on me a few years ago, he had any rights to tell me what the fuck to do. Granted, I was a grown ass man, but it still made me mad as fuck to think they had kept this shit a secret.

"Oh, you bad now? I'll hem yo' lil ass up, Judah. Don't fuckin' play with me, a'ight. You only got a glimpse of Supreme these couple weeks. I'ma give yo' ass the full effect, keep playin'." He snarled, pulling his pants up like his old ass was really 'bouta do something.

"I don't give a fuck who you is!"

"Oh my God! Judah, calm down!" My OG shouted, stepping between us. I had never disrespected my mama, but right now I wasn't trying to hear shit. I looked at her crazy as hell.

"I need to calm down? Y'all muthafuckas been lying to me all this fuckin' time and I'm supposed to calm down? Fuck outta here man!"

"Boy, I ain't gon' tell you no more-" Pree started, but I cut him off with a nasty right hook that would have stumbled anybody else, but his head barely turned. I ain't gon' lie, he ate that shit, but I still wasn't backing down. Not even after his nostrils flared and his eyes narrowed.

"Judah, what in the... get yo' ass outta here before the police come and I have to slap yo' ignant ass! Pree, move; we can handle this shit later!"

"Y'all ain't gotta handle shit with me, I'm good." I made sure to bump his ass hard as hell on my way out the door. What type of family keep shit like this a secret? I hated to leave my nigga Troy upstairs, but I would just have to come back and talk to him later. This shit was just too much to fucking handle.

* * *

IT HAD BEEN two months since I talked to my OG and Pree, and I was still going strong. Troy was doing better and going through physical therapy, so he could come home. I'd held off on killing Keys, so that my boy could be present when I did the honors. I wasn't too worried about him saying shit because he was scary as hell, but he was still going to die just to be on the safe side. Since I hadn't been fucking with my mama and shit, I had been spending all of my free time with Nivea and the kids, or Troy. If I wasn't with them, I was in the new studio that GMP had provided once I'd signed my contract. That's right, a nigga finally had settled down with a label, and they signed Troy's ass too. He was due to be released in the next two weeks. Just enough time for the party that GMP was throwing us. I was even set to perform the first track off my album, and I was real life excited. It was crazy how I wasn't able to share this moment with my OG, but I wasn't with that sneaky shit and honestly, I didn't know when I was gone be able to talk to them again. Nivea and the kids had filled the void I'd been missing though. I was starting to get used to being a family man. Shit was moving so good, I had planned on surprising them all with this five-bedroom house out in Olympia Fields. They had all had it rough since they found out Brenda and her bitch ass son were dead. It was hard faking like I felt bad about the situation, but they were better off without both of them, and they had me now anyways. They still went to see Quad occasionally, and I wasn't tripping about that, he knew what was up and he knew not to say or do no slick shit since I went up there. He ain't want no smoke with me for real though. Nigga knew about me, so he didn't have to ask.

"What's wrong, baby?" Nivea asked, looking up at me. She had turned into more than just my girl. She was becoming my everything and I confided in her about a lot of shit. She still worked for my mama and had been trying to convince me to talk to her, but I wasn't budging on that shit just yet.

"Nothin', just thinkin' 'bout how shit finna change."

"Awww, you nervous about the party and stuff, huh?" She smiled in the dark and snuggled closer to me.

"What? Hell nah! I'm ready to T up! Ain't shit to be nervous bout." I was more anxious to have the party than nervous. It was going to be at this new club called Exxpression and it was gone be all white. I couldn't wait to party with my shorty. Since she was a homebody and didn't like leaving the kids too much, we never really went to clubs together. I was trying to see her looking the same way she had that night I had to beat her baby daddy ass. That's one of the reasons I wanted it to be all white in the first place.

"You so damn cocky, Judah," she said, sucking her teeth.

"But you like that shit though. Now gimmie kiss and take yo' fine ass to sleep; you got class tomorrow." She puckered up her juicy ass lips, and I gave her two light pecks before giving her body a squeeze and closing my eyes. I had never slept more comfortable than with Nivea in my arms.

QUAD

1 week later...

I wasn't happy, and everyone around this bitch knew it. Not only was my mama and brother dead, but my baby mama was fucking the nigga who killed them. At first, I wasn't even going to sweat too hard about Nivea messing around with that little nigga. Although I didn't want nobody else in my pussy, it wasn't realistic to think that she was gone wait seven years for me. Besides that, I knew he wasn't gone last long with a woman like Nivea. She wasn't about that street shit that he lived and rapped about. Baby barely even listened to rap. Nah, I was gone let her think she was moving on and then when he cheated or left her for some Instagram model, I was gon' be right there waiting with open arms. The fact that he was the one who killed my family made him a target though, and I was still on the fence about whether or not Nivea would be too. See, about a week ago, some nigga that Jay used to hang with named Keys wrote me a letter explaining how Ju had held him at gunpoint and forced him to show him my mama crib. He said that was the day before they died, so he was basically telling me that he did it. Said it was because Jay had almost killed his mans, Troy, over some bullshit in the studio. Now while I knew my brother was a fucking idiot, did that mean he had to die? Should my mama have died for that shit? Besides Nivea, they were the only ones in my corner, and now since they were gone, and Nivea was getting her groove back and shit, all I had was Desiree. Little did they know that their happily ever after was about to be over with.

"Quad, you ready?" Desiree asked as she approached my cell. I grabbed the bag with my personal stuff in it and stepped closer to the bars.

"Stop askin' me stupid shit and let me up out this bitch!" I hissed irritably.

"You ain't gotta do all that." She smacked her lips. She was starting to get real mouthy behind these walls, and I couldn't wait until I was out of here so it wouldn't be C.O. and prisoner no more.

"Just let me out man." I wasn't in the mood to play with her. I still had to go and talk to these detectives one more time before they went and busted that nigga. She took her time with the keys 'cause she still had an attitude, and I was about ready to choke her dumb ass. She finally opened the gate and I made sure to step close to her so nobody could hear. "Stop fuckin' playing with me, Desiree, a'ight?"

I let her put the cuffs on me and snatch the bag I was carrying away. As I passed, niggas nodded and said their goodbyes, thinking that I was being transferred when in all actuality, I was being set free. I couldn't wait to see the look on Nivea's face when Ju's little ass got arrested, and she saw me in the world. He thought he was untouchable when he came up here popping off at me, but he was about to see I wasn't the roll over and die type of nigga.

When we made it outside, I squinted at how bright the sun was, but held my head back enjoying it anyway. It felt good to be free. Desiree uncuffed my hands and handed me her house key. "I'm gon' meet you at the house after my shift, okay?"

"Yeah, I'ma be there. Where else I'ma go?" I lied. I wanted to lay eyes on that nigga with my bitch, and I was hoping this interview didn't take long, so I could get to it.

"Right, well that's your ride." She pointed to a black SUV parked right out front. The tint was super dark, so I couldn't see inside but I knew it was the detectives. I made my way over and hopped into the still running car, appreciating the cool air that was blasting through that bitch.

"Y'all niggas ready 'cause I got shit to do?" I asked, rubbing my hands together like Birdman as we pulled off.

NIVEA

few days later
It was the night of Judah and Troy's party, and I was excited for my baby. Although he was still being stubborn about talking to his mama, he was making good on all of his promises and working hard on his album. He deserved this, and I was more than happy to share it with him. Him and Troy had been gone for most of the day getting ready while Niyah came over to help me. She was going to be Troy's arm candy for the night. They had met the other day when he was released from the hospital and hit it off right away. He ain't waste no time getting at her either. She said despite his tough exterior, he was sweet, and she was going to give him a chance.

"Stop moving before I burn you, Nivea, damn!" She snapped, staring at me through the mirror.

"Bitch, I wish you would burn me."

"You was just 'bouta be pullin' out that mommy pack you got and putting some cocoa butter on the back of yo' neck for real." She held up the curlers and said, but I waved her off.

"The day you burn me is the day you gone be eating a laxative cookie!" I warned. Niyah loved Jackie's cookies and always had me bringing her some whenever I worked. The way she was going, she was gone need a laxative from all the peanut butter in them.

"Now why would you mess with a bitch cookies, Niv? That's some cold shit." She tsked shaking her head and continuing to put wavy curls in my hair. I just shrugged.

"Well, stop playing with them curlers and we gone be good." She mumbled some smart shit under her breathe, but I noticed her hands got real steady.

Five minutes later, she was done, and I stood up so that I could slip on the diamond encrusted red bottoms that Judah had bought to match my white, sparkly Valentino dress. I turned and looked into the floor length mirror, twisting from side to side. Usually I shied away from super tight-fitting dresses, but I couldn't lie, I looked damn good. The ivory color looked amazing against my complexion, and I couldn't wait until Judah saw me

"Yessss bitch! You givin' me face and body, best friend!" Niyah said, hyping me up even more. She had done my makeup too with a smoky eye and some ombre red lips. We were definitely gone turn their party out with the way she was rocking her short, white Gucci romper with the heels that wrapped all the way up her calves to match. She had her hair in a high pony tail that grazed her lower back. She had kept her make up simple with a dramatic eye and some Spite Mac lip gloss.

"We gone be the baddest things in there," I quipped, giving her a high-five and flipping my hair over my shoulder.

"Don't be tryna be too bad. You know Ju don't play." I twisted my lips and shoo'ed her away.

"Judah is gone be on his best behavior."

"Yeah, until he sees you in that dress," she teased, snapping a picture. I wasn't going to pay her ass any attention. Judah had picked out the dress, so he already knew what it was gone look like.

"Whateva. Let's go, the car just pulled up," I told her, grabbing my clutch and keys quickly.

"Man, this dress lil as hell." Judah stressed an hour later after we had made our grand entrance. Niyah, who was right beside us, threw me a look, and I raised my middle finger.

"You picked this dress out, Judah. You knew what it was gon' look like," I said, pressing my body into his. He was looking so damn good in a white, short sleeve v-neck with some white Levi jeans and some spiked white Belenciaga's. I couldn't wait to get him home. Shit, I wanted to take him up to the bathrooms that they had for VIPs only.

"I know, but I ain't think you was gon' be pokin' out this muthafucka like this!" He groaned, throwing his head back. I wrapped my arms around his neck and pulled it back forward, planting a few quick kisses on his lips.

"That don't even matter, bae. Its only poking for you." He flashed his teeth and licked those juicy lips of his.

"Man, get a fuckin' room, my nigga," Troy's hating ass whined.

"I know right." Niyah added, and I gave them both the middle finger. They looked good standing there together. Troy had worn a white, collared shirt that he had left unbuttoned with a tank top underneath, and some white levis with white Gucci sneakers.

"You know I'm just playin', sis," he said, grinning, and I rolled my eyes playfully.

"Yeah, yeah, tell me anything," I teased.

Suddenly, the music went off and the DJ came over the mic loud as hell. "Ayeeee, how y'all feelin' tonight?" He questioned, and the crowd went wild. "Let me hear y'all make some noise for my niggas Ju Savage and Trigga Troy!"

Standing up in VIP, all eyes landed on us as they all clapped and cheered loudly. "I want y'all to show my nigga some love, a'ight! He 'bouta let y'all hear his first song off the album, give it up!" He shouted before motioning for Judah to come on stage. I looked at him confused because he didn't say he was performing tonight, and he smiled wide and gave me a kiss on the cheek.

"Be right back, shorty." He winked then disappeared out of our booth. Me and Niyah exchanged looks while Troy just stood there avoiding our glares.

When I heard Judah's voice come over the microphone, my attention instantly went to the stage, and I couldn't help but smile at his fine ass. All the ladies were out there screaming his name and acting crazy, but he kept his eyes on me.

"A while back, I did a lil something for my girl called the Nivea challenge. Y'all remember that?" He asked, and they all screamed out yes. "Good, good cause that one was important. That's why I went ahead and added it to the album. So tonight y'all gon' hear the full song!" He motioned for the DJ and a nice ass beat came through the speakers. "Real shit, shorty, this was the instrumental I was listening to when yo' ass fucked up my car," he said, gaining a laugh out of everybody. "I was supposed to be making a track for the ladies and then boom, yo ass hit my shit. So, what better way to honor me meeting you than to put words to the background music that started it all, right?"

By now, I had tears coming down my face as Judah began to rap about how we met, and every stage we'd been through all the way up until now. I dabbed at my face hoping that I hadn't fucked up my make up too bad as Niyah nudged my arm grinning widely.

"Awww, best friend!" She gushed.

"Aye, bae, come here right quick." Judah motioned for me

once the final note had played. I was stuck in place until Niyah's rude ass hit me on the shoulder roughly, snapping me out of my thoughts.

"Bitch, go get yo man!"

That was all it took for me to run as fast as the high ass heels I was wearing allowed. I'd just cleared the stage and reached Judah when shrieks rang out through the club, drawing everyone's attention to the stream of police storming through and making their way to where me and Judah stood on stage.

"What the fuck, man?" He said, moving me out of the way to stand behind him.

"Judah Thompson, we got a warrant for your arrest for the murder of one Quajay, and Brenda Mitchell." The detective who had led them in said with a slick smirk.

"Ahh hell nah, what the fuck you mean? My boy ain't killed nobody!" Troy shouted, pushing his way through to where we stood.

"Oh my God! What's going on, Judah!" I cried, grabbing ahold of his arm. That was Quad's mama and brother that they were accusing him of killing.

"Bae, I swear these niggas lying. I ain't did shit!" He pleaded as I backed away.

The detective pulled out his cuff and roughly grabbed Judah up before he could reach for me. I watched in horror as they dragged him away kicking and screaming through the crowd of angry club goers. Troy followed behind them barking orders and demanding that somebody call Mone. Niyah came out of nowhere and wrapped her arms around me as I cried. I was stunned and confused, not knowing what to do. Had Judah really been the one that had killed my kids' grandma and uncle?

* * *

"DON'T BELIEVE THAT SHIT, Nivea. I can already see the wheels spinning in yo' head." Niyah told me once we were back at my apartment. I paced the floor as she sat on the couch watching me trying to play detective in my mind. There was no way that he had come over here after committing two murders. I covered my mouth in horror thinking about him touching me and knowing what he'd done.

"Nivea, I swear to God, calm down!" She said when pounding at my door froze us both in place.

"That's probably the people downstairs 'cause you makin' so much damn noise!" Niyah went and checked the door. "Oh shit, Nivea!" I rushed to the door to see what was going on now and stopped in my tracks at the sight of Quad at my door.

"What's up, baby mama?"

To be continued..........